VENOM KISSED

VENOM KISSED

SYDNEY WINWARD

Venom Kissed

Cover art by Cangxxx Graphics

Published by Silver Forge Books

Paperback 978-1-960461-07-0

http://www.sydneywinward.com

To the racing clock. I got this story done on time!

BOOKS BY SYDNEY WINWARD

The Bloodborn Series

Bloodborn

Bloodbond

Bloodscourge

Bloodbane

Bloodcurse

Bloodheir

Sunlight and Shadows Series

A Breath of Sunlight

A Taste of Shadows

A Glimpse of Music

A Kiss of Embers

A Balm of Healing

Letters to Love Series

Yours, Sterling

Forever, Mirabelle

Always, Ivette

Charles, With Love

Lord Death Series

A Waltz with Lord Death

Novellas

Through Wylder Meadows

Root Brew Float

On Silver Wings

Bloodmoon

Bloodvow

Selkie

Venom Kissed

CHAPTER *One*

WHAT COLOR WAS the sky?

Much time had passed since Kikka Takasi had last seen the vast outdoors. The moon hanging in the sky. The lazy clouds floating over a large blue canvas. The wind blowing softly in the trees. Years ago, she'd forgotten what the faces of her family looked like. And now? She found herself slowly losing the memory of the sky.

Because the sky represented freedom. And Kikka feared she would never be free again.

The chains clamped around her wrists rattled with her movement as she struggled to sit, wincing when her weakened body burned and ached. All she wanted was to lie down and give up. But she refused to abandon hope. Even when hope had seemingly died the moment her family had turned her in for their own gain.

She had nothing else. No one else.

And she likely never would.

Water dripped from the ceiling, her sensitive ears picking up the splash somewhere in the darkness surrounding her. A faint scream echoed down the dank corridor outside the cell, the thick metal bars separating her from the other cells, from freedom.

Her beast rolled, stretching within her, signaling the start of another torturous night. Black and gray patterns slithered across her skin from her wrists, up her arms, to her neck. Her eyes transitioned from green to yellow with a faint prickling sensation, marking the beginning of another dusk.

Suddenly, the darkness appeared lighter as her beast's vision amplified the dim interior of her prison cell. Water dribbled down cracked, stone walls. Gouge marks in the hard rock revealed many hard nights and desperate attempts at escape. She sniffed the air, making out the scent of dirt, mildew, and blood.

Fangs elongated in her mouth. Her fingernails lengthened and curled into sharp, black claws. Her back threatened to rip open to continue the rest of her transformation, but she managed to control her beast enough to stop it.

They wanted her to transform. *They* wanted to mutilate her. To take what was not theirs. But no matter how miserable they made her life, her beast was the only thing she had left. And she would protect her to her last breath.

She took several deep breaths to calm her inner beast, to resist the remainder of the transformation. Scaled patterns continued crawling across her skin, slower this time, as its dejected spirit fell as one with hers.

Footsteps slapped against damp stone, alerting her to someone's approach.

She hissed as her ears picked up the jangle of keys, and she scrambled backward into the darkest corner of the cell, as far as her chains allowed.

Another hiss of pain escaped her when the metal dug into her wrists. But the pain was preferable to wherever they planned to take her.

One of her captors appeared moments later, his eyes dark and menacing as he unlocked her cell door. He wore thick leather armor over his entire body, a double layer over his hands and arms. She'd bitten him once before. But she'd been starved for so long that she no longer produced venom.

"Time to go," he said in a growly voice as he reached for her.

But right as he touched the chains, she darted forward within inhuman speed and sank her fangs into his leg. But rather than breaking through flesh, her fangs met the resistance of his leather armor.

The flash of his hand struck her in the face, hard enough for her to release him. Next, his boot kicked her in the stomach, her body smashing against the cold stone wall. A heavy, silent breath escaped her lips as pain flared in her body. Her beast rattled and hissed within her, threatening to transform for a fight neither of them could win when weakness plagued them. Rather than trying to attack again, she instead focused her attention on reining back her beast as it fought against the cages of her willpower.

He unlocked the shackles securing her chains to the wall, and without the added support from her restraints, her body thumped exhaustedly to the ground.

No more. Please, no more.

With her wrists still shackled together, the man latched onto the chain and dragged her out of her cell. She barely managed to keep her feet beneath her when his long stride outmatched her weak gait. Her bare feet scraped against damp, rough stone. Her ragged clothing snagged on limestone mortar jutting unevenly from stacked stone walls.

He dragged her past empty cells, down darkened hallways, and up large steps as tall as her knees. She stumbled on the first one, scraping her legs when she fell. But then the man heaved her back onto her feet and continued down another dank corridor that smelled of rot and…

She inhaled sharply as her senses picked up the gentle caress of a soft, *fresh* breeze, the whisper of wind whistling down the prison hallway. And then her mouth dropped open when he yanked her *outside* into the chilly winter air of midnight.

A foggy breath escaped her mouth as she spotted stars high above in the night sky. But just as she searched desperately for the moon, the man shoved her into a cart, her view of the stars obscured by thick metal slats surrounding each side of her.

She hadn't seen the sky in ten years. It was more beautiful than she remembered.

The back doors of the cart slammed closed, and moments later, it lurched forward as the horses started their journey down the road.

Kikka's serpent eyes quickly adjusted to the darkness to find six other occupants in the metal cart with her, each like her.

A monster.

Three were *others* with sharp teeth and tails like blades. One was a young ent. Two were bird-women, one with her feathers plucked from her pockmarked skin and the other still boasting gold and red feathers, her expression bright and cheery.

A newcomer. They never remained optimistic for long. She was never going to retain her feathers when her captors were done with her.

"What was your crime?" the golden bird-woman asked as she nudged Kikka in the leg.

Kikka flinched away, hugging her knees to her chest and refusing to look the woman in the eye. It only ended badly when they interacted with each other. And who was the easiest person to punish?

The monster who scared them the most.

"She doesn't speak," the sapling named Aspen answered, her body made of the bark and branches of a young ent still growing slowly when she couldn't attach her roots to the ground.

"Why not?"

When the reminder of her affliction tore her heart in two, she buried her face into her knees to try to avoid further notice. Although her eyes burned, tears didn't fall. She'd already cried years' worth of tears within the first few weeks of captivity alone.

However, she still heard the sapling answer in a hushed voice. "They tried to cut out her beast at the throat. She won't speak because she can't."

Kikka swallowed the lump of emotion lodged in her maimed throat. They'd taken so much from her by stealing her voice.

"How repulsive! They think they can cut it out? Why would they want it?"

"She's a shifter. They do it to all of them. And they haven't stopped because they've succeeded in cleaving the beast from its host with other shifters." The sapling lowered her voice even more, and even though Kikka covered her ears to block out the sound, her serpent hearing caught it, anyway. "The host dies, but the king keeps the beasts to fight in his wars."

She hissed. Or perhaps her beast did. They were one of the same but separate simultaneously.

Her beast had emerged at only eleven years old, but she wished more than anything it had never emerged at all. All it had ever caused her was heartache and suffering.

The faintest flash of light drew her attention to a small crevice between two metal slats in the cart. She peered through the crack and barely made out the passage of white powder, dismal brown buildings, and another cart falling into line behind them on the road.

Turning to the sapling, she pointed to the crack, a question in her eyes. *Where are we going?*

"The king's palace," the other woman answered with a dejected frown. "I overheard *them* talking. They plan to try more severe experiments on us."

Kikka squeezed her eyes shut and released a long, tortured breath. Ten years she'd been a prisoner. Ten years she'd survived experiment after experiment, a variety of different methods of torture.

She did not think she could endure any more.

The horses pulling their metal prison whinnied as they halted abruptly with a jarring jolt. And then screams lifted in the air amidst war cries, steel smashing against steel as if two different parties were fighting.

Fear crashed into her as she hugged the metal wall, eyes wide.

"What was that?" Aspen gasped.

The fire-bird answered with a grin. "Our rescue."

CHAPTER *Two*

WARREN STEELSWORN CROUCHED in the boughs of a tree bereft of leaves, watching the three metal boxes pulled by horses below with a careful eye. Two of his friends, Gael and Koa, attacked the first convoy, fighting against the monster slavers with skillful, practiced hands. Weapon fought against weapon, steel striking against steel.

Cornered by several enemies, Aiden blasted them with a spark of white magic called their *iskra*. The magic slammed into the men, but some of it smashed into the second convoy behind them. The large, metal structure tipped precariously on its wheels before thudding back onto the ground. The weight of the box broke one of the wheels off. And then the jarring impact cracked the lock in two.

The metal door crashed open, and several monster-like creatures flooded outside. Some made a quick escape. Others stayed to fight, making quick work of the enemy even with chains clamped around their wrists, roots, or fins.

The third convoy turned around on the path, frantically fleeing from the attack farther ahead.

Warren's mouth twitched with smug satisfaction moments before the convoy passed beneath the tree.

He leaped down from a thick branch and onto the metal box, denting the roof with his weight. The horses whinnied in fright, sprinting down the path faster when the driver frantically snapped the reins. He nearly lost his balance and toppled off, but he reached deep within himself for his *iskra* and secured his feet to the convoy with a pool of white light beneath his boots.

Two men on horseback thundered down the road on either side of the convoy, looming closer with each passing second. One of them unsheathed a sword, standing in his stirrups as he swiped at Warren.

Gritting his teeth, he released his magic long enough to jump over the blade mid-air. But by doing so, the convoy shifted forward beneath him. He lost his footing on icy metal as he struggled to remain on top.

His feet slipped. He cried out moments before he managed to grasp onto the side of the metal box, using his magic to hold him securely.

His nostrils flared at the effort it took to keep himself from letting go. If they lost even one convoy, their mission would be a failure. His friends were inside the metal prisons. Friends and helpless creatures who needed aid.

And he refused to give up on them.

When his feet couldn't find purchase on the slick convoy, he instead allowed himself to slip a fraction until he got a good view of the horses' legs galloping down the road.

Iskra pooled in his hands, and when enough power gathered at his fingertips, he blasted a stream of calm at the horses. The magic soothed them enough to slow their gait from a gallop to a trot, and finally to a slow walk.

Warren ducked beneath the blade of one of his enemies, releasing the convoy and landing on his feet. The driver attempted to snap the reins to encourage the horses to run, but they refused his orders under the influence of his calming *iskra*.

Both riders swung down from their mounts and met him in combat. Blade smashed against blade as they circled him, taking turns in trying to cut him down with their weapons.

He spun back and forth between his opponents, parrying sword against sword, dodging attack after attack. His blade moved swiftly through the air, blocking stabs and swipes until one of the men misstepped.

Warren took advantage of the opening and thrust his sword straight through the man's unguarded chest. He yanked it back out and ducked the swing of the next man's blade.

As they traded blow after blow, Warren admitted the man was a great warrior. But the reminder of what he'd done to innocent, defenseless *others* gave him the strength to advance until he was on the offense. The other man tried in vain to keep up with his swift movements.

He backed his opponent into a snowbank, trapping him between the large icy structure and a boulder blocking his path.

In two powerful swings, he disarmed the man and quickly struck him down, the snow bleeding red beneath him.

The driver of the prison carriage leaped to the ground and tried to flee, but Warren was faster. In a few strides, he caught up to him, grabbed him by the collar, and slammed him against the side of the coach.

"Give me the key to unlock it," Warren growled in the man's face.

None of these men were innocent. They'd enslaved and tortured helpless individuals. His group had been searching for them for a long time. They'd only managed to find them by having one of their own get purposefully captured to lead them to the den.

"You don't know what's in there!" the man cried as Warren held him by the throat, pinned against the metal container.

He lifted his lips and snarled, showing off the sharp canines in his mouth, each filed to a point to mimic fangs. "Oh, I know exactly what lies within. And *you* are the most monstrous thing here."

Not giving the sick bastard any more time to beg for his life, he snapped the man's neck and tossed him into a pile of powdery snow on the side of the road. And then...

All was quiet.

He lifted his head to find they hadn't traveled too far from the other convoys. He glanced toward his friends—Gael, Aiden, and Koa—as each cleaned their weapons and searched the pockets of the fallen prison masters for keys to open the mobile steel cells. Gael found a set of keys in the trousers pocket of one of the fallen men and tossed one his way. He caught it deftly in the air.

And then taking a deep breath to steel himself for what he might find inside the container… He fit the key inside the lock and turned it. The door creaked open slowly. And taking him by surprise, the first to fly out was Cyra, his fire-bird friend, as she flapped her red and gold wings and embraced him tight around the waist with feathery arms.

"Oh, I'm so glad you found us! You had me worried for a bit." Her sister, Enara, appeared behind her—a bird-woman with black feathers like a raven. The very woman they had staged this rescue for.

Or at least, she used to have black feathers only weeks ago before her capture.

He swallowed the hard lump in his throat when he noticed her pocked skin, as if someone had plucked each of the feathers out of her body. Her expression was withdrawn, her mouth twisted in pain.

He carefully helped her out of the mobile prison and set her on top of a horse with Aiden. Guilt punched him in the gut as his gaze trailed her languid movements. If only they'd been faster, if only they'd watched out for her better, then she never would have been caught by the slavers to begin with.

Just like Astrid…

He quickly shook the terrible memory away.

Several *others* filed out of the metal box, and just when he thought it was empty, Cyra peeked her head inside the cart and smiled at someone who remained inside. "You're safe now. They're my friends."

Still, the person refused to emerge, at least until Cyra coaxed a little bit more for the woman to crane her neck and peek outside.

Warren's heart caught at her tortured, ragged appearance. The clothes on her body were threadbare, ripped in many places and barely hanging on thin limbs. Dirt marred every exposed piece of her skin, including her face and hair. The only thing it didn't touch were her yellow eyes. But even then, distrust and fear radiated from the thin black slits of her pupils as her gaze darted back and forth as if she expected someone to grab her.

He dared to move a little closer, wanting—no, *needing*—her to understand he was there to help. That she was not alone. He and his friends would take care of her.

The woman flinched away as he advanced slowly, but when he revealed the key in his hand, her gaze darted to his face to show the surprise in her expression.

She allowed him to approach, even as her hands shook as he held onto her thin wrist to keep her steady as he unlocked the first shackle and then the second.

The chains holding her captive fell to the ground with a *thunk*.

For a long moment, she stared at the chains as if in disbelief, as if unable to comprehend her freedom. Some of the other captives escaped into the night to return to whatever they'd called home before getting captured. However, some of them, especially the weaker of them, planned to stay. But this woman?

What would she choose?

Warren wrapped a blanket around her thin frame, and when she didn't protest, he lifted her out of the prison and into his arms.

"You're safe now," he murmured reassuringly. "No one can ever hurt you again."

She clung tight to him around the neck, burying her face into his shoulder. And when she quickly relaxed against him, he realized she'd fallen asleep.

He shared a melancholy look with Cyra, who had been like a sister to him for most of his life. What had this poor woman gone through? How long had she been enslaved?

"Let's get back to the fortress!" he called to the others just as Koa detached the horses from the prison carriages and set them free to go their own way. They didn't need the king hunting them down over a few stolen horses. They were already in deep enough trouble taking his captives. "We want to be off the roads when someone discovers what happened here."

Careful not to jostle the sleeping woman, he mounted his own destrier. The large horse towered over everyone else, its sleek, black fur glinting beneath the moonlight overhead. The rescued prisoners mounted extra horses they'd brought, two to a horse. Each *other* appeared close to collapsing as it was. He didn't want to make any of them walk if they could help it.

Glancing one last time down the road to make sure no other carts had made the journey with the other three, he turned his mount in the direction of the mountains.

Their group made haste, first through the harsh terrain of traveling off the beaten path to hide their tracks. Next, they braved crossing a frozen lake a few of them at a time to further disguise their footsteps. And finally, they found the trail leading over the pass and through the mountains.

Warren glanced at the people behind him before his gaze slowly moved to the front of the group, counting how many had decided to make the journey to their safe haven. Twelve *others* and four from his original team.

The *others* appeared ragged with exhaustion heavy in their expressions. Many had been mutilated in some way, such as his friend, Enara, whose feathers had been plucked from her body. Or a sapling whose leaves were absent, the branches of her arm twisted in such a way that he wasn't sure she would ever recover from such mistreatment.

He hoped more than anything that these people could heal from their experience as captives. The first step was removing them from harm and rehoming them in a safe, comforting environment. The rest was up to them.

His grip tightened on the woman in his arms, his subconscious seemingly trying to find a way to protect her even when no danger presented itself. He wasn't sure why he was already more protective of her than the others. Perhaps because she'd chosen him to keep her safe.

It made him feel…

Special.

Finally, after traveling through the snowy pass, the sky lightened little by little with the coming dawn, enough for him to spot their fortress hugging the side of the mountain up ahead.

The large structure was made of stone bricks and several levels of turrets, balconies, and a long parapet used as a lookout to keep them safe from outside threats.

As they approached, one of the *others* who acted as a soldier, a wolf shifter named Eldon, opened the metal gates and admitted them entrance.

Although the grounds were currently covered in snow, the front yard, as they liked to call it, was usually teeming with a variety of flowers and fruit trees. The stables were lined up on the west side of the wall while a greenhouse rested on the eastern side of the fortress. They were self-sustaining, even during the winter months, and able to provide for a great number of people. Everyone worked together to pitch in with their own talents so they all could thrive.

Warren dismounted with the woman still in his arms, nodding his head to the stable master—a man with the head of a cat and talons like a bird. And then he started toward the fortress with the others in tow, only to startle when he found the woman in his arms with her eyes wide open, taking in her surroundings, and especially the *others*, with wonder in her expression.

For a moment, he couldn't help but stare. Earlier, he could have sworn her eyes had been yellow. But now, they were green, and her nails were short like a human's rather than long and curved with a wicked black glint.

The moment they entered the fortress, a wave of warmth washed over him, emanating from the billowing hearth in the common area filled with tables and chairs for conversation and relaxation. The kitchens were through another set of doors, as well as the mess hall where over two hundred of them took their meals each day.

Without another moment's delay, he exited the commons with a couple other women following at his heels. They walked down a long corridor with a door at the end leading to the backyard training barracks. Rather than entering the outdoors, he climbed a staircase to the left leading to the upper floors filled with dozens of bed chambers. Most of them shared a room with two or three other people, unless there were married couples, in which they shared one together. They usually placed the newcomers in their own rooms for the first few days to acquaint them with their new home without fear of threat or harm.

He entered one such room with a large wooden tub filled with water in the middle of the chamber while a bed and clothing chest rested on the other.

But as he tried to set the woman down, she only clung tighter to him, her breaths escaping rapidly from her mouth as if on the verge of panic.

"You're safe here," he reassured, not for the first time. "These kind women will help you bathe and dress."

The woman shook her head and pointed to his chest.

He glanced self-consciously at the two waiting women, one a cat shifter and the other a dog shifter, each currently in their human forms. Sure, he often helped the new *others* find their place here. But to bathe them? Dress them?

Of course, he wasn't married, nor did he have anyone special in his life. But…

Finally, he nodded to the women. "I'll help her today, and you two will help her tomorrow."

They shuffled out of the room and closed the door behind them. Even alone with him, the woman didn't look at him with fear, but rather with relief. And only then did she allow him to set her down on her feet.

However, she quickly stumbled, catching herself on the edge of the tub. He frowned when he noticed the scabbed-over scrapes on her legs, as if she'd been dragged over rough terrain before her rescue.

"I'll turn my back as you undress," he said, concerned when she still didn't speak.

He rummaged through the wooden chest on the opposite side of the room and located a woman's dress a lilac and cream in color with purple ribbons decorating the sleeves and bodice. It looked as if it might fit her. But then again, he wasn't the greatest judge of clothing.

He set out the dress, underthings, stockings, and boots on top of the bed before turning back to the tub to find her curled in a ball within it, chin resting on her knees.

"What's your name?" he asked in a calm, even voice in an attempt to remain unthreatening to her.

She didn't answer, the poor thing still frightened from the terrifying ordeal of her enslavement.

"My name is Warren." He snatched a piece of soap from beside the tub and handed it to her. But her shaky fingers quickly dropped it in the water.

Rather than trying to make her attempt it a second time, he grabbed the fallen soap and silently asked with raised brows if she was all right with him helping. After a moment of staring back at him, she finally nodded.

"There you are," Warren murmured comfortingly as he gently scrubbed her dirtied back with the bar of soap, rubbing her chafed skin as gently as possible while trying to help get her clean.

From how it appeared, she likely hadn't had a proper bath in…well, a very long time. The water quickly turned brown like mud when several layers of dirt clung to her skin.

When she didn't protest his gentle treatment of her, he continued to scrub the soap in slow circles from her neck to her shoulders, down her arms…

His jaw clenched when what had previously been a dirty captive turned into a *woman* before his eyes. Long neck. Slender arms. Small shoulders. And *curves*. Though, he tried to keep his attention on the soap in his hand rather than the lather washing away the dirt to reveal more and more of soft, supple skin.

The woman continued to hunch in the water, which effectively hid her more intimate areas. He was glad for it. He could handle a simple washing. But that was before he knew what lay beneath the dirt.

Taking a deep breath to distract himself from his roaming thoughts, he scrubbed the soap through the dirt-covered locks of her hair. She sighed as if the motion relieved her scalp of pain or pressure.

And then he guided her head backward with the intent to wash the soap away with a bucket of water.

But he gasped when he noticed the scar starting at her throat and climbing down her neck to the middle of her chest and to her belly. It was an incision. Perhaps even multiple incisions. As if they'd tried to cut her open several different times.

She hunched tighter into a ball as if to hide the scar from him. But it was too late. He'd already seen it.

His fist clenched as anger coursed through him. His blood boiled to realize just how much she had suffered at the hands of the men they'd killed. He only wished they could have found her sooner to prevent her from enduring such agony.

"Close your eyes," he managed to instruct in a soft tone despite the fury threatening to explode from his *iskra*.

He scooped a bucketful of water and dumped it over her head, effectively cleaning the mud from her hair and scalp to reveal the brown hair hiding beneath it. It was a lighter shade than his own, and longer than his shoulder-length curls, though it was too soon to tell exactly what color it would dry to.

Thankfully, she managed to clean her more intimate areas as he turned to face the door, his back to her. He heard a brief splash, followed by the soft padding of feet.

"Head on down to the kitchen for something to eat if you are able. If not, someone will bring something to you. Supper will also be served in the mess hall later tonight."

No answer.

With a frown, he opened the door and slipped into the hallway, wondering why the woman refused to speak to him.

At least until he inhaled sharply at the sudden realization. He recalled the scars at her throat. Perhaps she didn't speak because she was physically unable to.

His previous fury returned with a vengeance as he stomped down the hallway, his expression contorted in a scowl. The men responsible were all dead, but it wasn't enough justice for what had been done to their prisoners.

He jogged down the stairs and entered the commons where more newcomers rested from the long journey to the fortress. He searched the vicinity for Enara, but Cyra must have taken her sister to their room.

Behind him, Gael clapped him on the shoulder, a smile stretching the long scar hidden halfway beneath his bearded face. "The snake girl, eh? I heard you heartily volunteered to bathe her."

Warren rolled his eyes and shoved his friend away. "I don't do romantic relationships. You can force the notion up your arse."

Subconsciously, his fingers stroked the golden chain hanging around his neck with a yellow feather attached, reminding him why he rescued *others*. Each one of his friends had different reasons for doing what they did, and he was no different.

He was only grateful he wasn't alone.

But even then, he couldn't help the pull of his thoughts to the young serpent woman. It was best he kept his distance from her. He couldn't afford to get close to *anyone*. Not again.

And perhaps not ever.

CHAPTER
Three

A SCOWL RESTED on Kikka's face as she berated herself for her terrified demeanor. For cowering in corners and flinching away from others. She knew she was safe here. She felt it in her heart.

Then why did fear still plague her?

Perhaps because when she closed her eyes, all she saw was darkness, cruelty, and flashes of pain. Perhaps because when she was surrounded by silence, all she heard were screams, rattling chains, and the viscous snarls of men with weapons.

I don't have to be afraid anymore, she reassured herself.

A rattle sounded in her ears as her beast slithered through her body, its gray pattern weaving across her skin. *We likes him,* it murmured in a hiss-like voice inside her head.

Kikka didn't refute her beast because she knew it to be true. Warren was kind and gentle, and most of all, he felt *safe.*

Another rattle, but one that sounded more like a contented purr. *Why don't we sssay hello?*

The insinuation didn't go over her head. If the beast had her way, there would be more than just a simple hello.

We are maimed, she reminded her beast as she crossed the room on weak, shaky legs and grimaced at the frilly dress lying on the bed. It reminded her of who she had been in a past life before her captivity. She hated the reminder. *He won't look twice at us.*

She picked up the frock, her frown deepening as she turned it from front to back to inspect the entirety of it. Yes, she was grateful for something to wear other than rags. But did it have to be *this*?

Tossing the garment aside, she sluggishly knelt down and dug into the chest filled with clothes and shoes, second-hand if she had to venture a guess. Many of the items of clothing were far more beautiful than anything she'd worn in the past ten years.

But nothing was quite right.

Her heart jumped, excitement alighting within her as she spotted black leather at the bottom of the chest. The trousers looked as if they might have belonged to a boy at one point. But it had pockets and several places to strap on weapons.

Of course, she had no weapons training. Neither did she own any weapons. But she never wanted to be defenseless again if she could help it. First, she needed to find something to protect herself in the first place.

She pulled on the trousers, her beast rattling happily when they fit as if she were always meant to wear them. Next, she found a black, sleeveless leather vest that cinched together in the front, leather straps secured over her shoulders. She frowned at the way it revealed a good portion of her scar. But no matter what she wore, at least some of it would be visible. And she didn't want to hide. She wanted to *live*.

Long, black claws emerged from the tips of her fingers, and she used the sharp points to cut the fabric of the vest until it fit her perfectly like her trousers. And finally, she pulled on the boots before collapsing onto the bed when she gasped for breath, exhaustion consuming every part of her body.

She needed food and water to satisfy her beast and give her the energy she needed to keep going, to move forward.

But how could she brave the strangers within the fortress?

She didn't get the opportunity to answer her own question when she fell into a deep sleep and woke only for a short time when someone brought food to her room. She ate ravenously before curling into a ball and sleeping for what felt like days. It had been so long since she'd slept on anything but a hard, dirty floor. The cot was heavenly in comparison.

When she woke a second time, she blinked her eyes against the confusing disorientation of finding her room growing darker rather than lighter. She stretched her aching limbs and sluggishly crossed the room to gaze out the window.

Her breath caught when she saw the entire valley from her vantage point. Purple mountains and hills covered in white snow stretched across the landscape. From here, she spotted the lake they had traveled across, most of it obscured by a layer of fresh powder. And then she watched in awe as winged *others* flew across the skies overhead as if they hadn't a care in the world.

Thinking of her own suppressed wings, she desperately wanted to join them, to remember what it had been like to fly before she'd quickly been thrown into captivity.

Another sigh of contentment escaped her lips as she gazed into skies slowly transitioning into the pinks, yellows, and oranges of dusk. She had forgotten the beautiful splendor that was the sky. It was one of the things she had missed the most about her old life.

After a few minutes of admiring the view, she took a deep, calming breath and hesitantly crossed the room. She took another breath before she opened the door, peering into the hallway. Her serpent hearing caught several murmured voices behind the doors nearest her, and she spotted the flicker of a blue skirt before the woman slammed her door closed behind her.

Let me out, her serpent hissed. Her beast could make an appearance before dusk if she wanted to, but she mostly became active at night. She had not fully released her beast in many years. It had never been safe.

Not yet.

She didn't mention that she wanted Warren to see *her* before seeing her beast, but by the way it hissed and rattled with discontentment, her beast was not happy with being suppressed for a moment longer.

To her disappointment, as Kikka wandered the many hallways, she never ran into Warren. Surely, he must be tired after their daring rescue. Perhaps he was sleeping behind closed doors.

Therefore, she occupied herself with learning the turns and bends in the hallways within the fortress, including the many rooms, big and small, inside the large structure. The decor was far from fancy despite the large fortress, but it felt homey, filled with jesting and laughter and *happiness.* The people here were happy. And she so desperately wanted that for herself.

After finding a path leading downstairs, she delighted when she peeked her head inside a weapons and armory room filled with all kinds of swords, daggers, knives, and more. Unfortunately, the room wasn't empty, but rather occupied by three men and two women.

One of the men with short blond hair and earrings climbing one of his ears noticed her and grinned as he casually rested his hand against the sword at his belt. "You're one of the new *others*, aren't you?" He snapped his fingers. "The snake girl." When she said nothing, of course, he crossed the room, picked up two daggers, and held them out to her. "You wanna try?"

She nodded enthusiastically and took the daggers from him. They were a bit smaller than the ones he'd previously been practicing with, but they fit nicely in her hands. She swiped them through the air, and the man laughed, holding his hands up as if to defend himself.

"Whoa there! Try not to take someone's eye out." He ran his fingers through his hair, his eyes flashing from brown to a dark orange. A wolf shifter, perhaps.

Her gaze darted to his throat, wondering if he, too, had been mutilated like herself. But there was no such scar.

"The name's Eldon." He held out a hand, but she cautiously shied away from him. She knew nothing about him. She didn't know if he was safe.

Continuing, he asked, "Wanna sit with me at supper?"

He's not afraid of me…

Not knowing how else to communicate, she shrugged her shoulders apologetically. She wasn't ready for…whatever he was offering.

"Keep them," he said, nodding toward the daggers. "You won't need them here. But it's better having them."

Thanking him with a nod, she sheathed the daggers and tucked them into her belt before setting off toward the mess hall at a brisk pace. Being near people simultaneously made her feel safe and uncomfortable at the same time. But thus far, no one had tried to attack her. And now with her new daggers on her person, at least she had a fighting chance to defend herself should the need arise.

Her mouth salivated long before she caught the scent of hearty food wafting down the hallway. The beast within her rattled and slithered with excitement, and she couldn't help but increase her pace.

But then she froze before entering the commons when she spotted two men wearing armor, each standing before the hearth with arms crossed, speaking in hushed tones.

All too suddenly, her throat dried as she recognized one of them as Warren. His loose brown curls brushed against his shoulders, shadowed scruff dotting his jaw. The blue of his eyes was barely visible beneath the dim light of the room, but they were filled with the passion of determination.

She hugged the wall as her gaze traveled from the roots of his brown hair to his broad shoulders and muscled arms to the dirt on his black boots. He exuded confidence in the way he stood, in the way he held himself as if ready to fight at the drop of a pin. The curls of his hair frame his strong, sturdy jaw. And his lips… Unlike the rest of him, they appeared soft and gentle, almost as if they might curve into a smile at any moment.

Her stomach fluttered inside her, her heart racing at the mere sight of him. He was a handsome man.

She pushed away from the wall and craned her neck for a better view of the hand that brushed a strand of hair out of his face. His fingers were bare. Perhaps he was not married, but it didn't mean he was unattached.

The man beside Warren—Gael—lifted his head to reveal the faint pink scar stretched across his face from eyebrow to jaw when he noticed her standing beside the wall. His eyes snapped open wide, his mouth hanging agape. "By the nine!" he hissed, not seeming to realize she could hear him. "What a beauty!" He elbowed Warren in the ribs. "You lucky dog. Look who's been watching you."

Mortification climbed her neck in the form of blistering heat as Warren turned his head in her direction. His eyes quickly locked with hers before surprise lifted his brows as his gaze swept down her body, taking her in.

Her long, light brown hair had dried in voluminous waves down her back, framing her heart-shaped face. Dirt no longer marred her skin. And for once in ten years, she felt beautiful.

Bashfulness overcame her as she ducked behind the wall and started down the hallway at a brisk pace. Her beast prodded her to turn back, to brave her fears and confront the strange feelings taking flight in her heart. But she was terrified. And she didn't understand why.

"Wait!" Warren called after her, startling her into spinning around.

He trotted toward her, and she backed up until her shoulders brushed against the cold stone wall behind her. She lowered her gaze to the ground when she reminded herself she was maimed. No man would want her when she could not speak.

He stepped closer until his large frame loomed over her. The earthy musk of his scent entered her nostrils, spinning her thoughts until she found it difficult to latch onto anything other than *want, need.* Rather than feeling trapped and cornered, her beast rattled so loudly with desire that he seemed to hear it, as he stepped backward in a defensive manner. Her cheeks filled with heat, surprising her, as she hadn't thought it was possible to feel any more embarrassed than she already was.

"I don't mean to make you feel threatened," he said in the soothing tone she enjoyed so much. "I will keep my distance if it pleases you."

She shook her head, not knowing how to communicate that it was not fear she felt.

A breathy laugh escaped him as he took that single step forward once more. "I still don't know your name. Are you able to help me out?"

Kikka's mouth quirked to the side as she finally lifted her gaze. She bent her fingers and held them in a triangular shape over her head to try to convey her name.

"Cat," he guessed. When she shook her head, he ventured, "Kitty?"

Her lips pressed together with the frustration of not being able to communicate. A long time ago, she'd learned a little bit of how to read and write. But over the years, she'd forgotten everything, and now couldn't even spell her own name no matter how hard she tried to recall the letters that formed each sound.

Oh! she mouthed as she mimicked taking a key from her pocket and unlocking a door.

"Lock." He scratched his chin when she again shook her head. "Key?"

Her entire expression lit up at the sound of the first part of her name from his lips. She held up two fingers to indicate for him to say it twice.

"Keykey."

She tipped her hand back and forth to say he was close. And then she dipped her finger down and up, opening her mouth to form what would have been an "uh" sound.

After a moment of furrowing his brows, his eyes lit up as he seemed to figure out what she tried to express. "Kikka."

Relief washed through her as she nodded enthusiastically. How many years had passed since she'd heard her own name? Since her identity had been stripped from her with the end of a blade?

But now she wanted it back. She was free. And she planned to live her life rather than allow it to pass her by.

"What a beautiful name." He smiled, and for a moment, the sight startled her when fangs peeked out from the bottom of his upper lip.

When words couldn't do her justice, she allowed her own fangs to slip down the slightest bit to mimic the length of his, and then she tipped her head to the side questioningly. Was he a vampire? Or a snake shifter like her?

As if reading her thoughts, he shook his head. "Just a human. It's a long story." He lifted a single eyebrow and held out his arm to her. "Will you allow me to escort you to supper? The long way, of course."

He smiled teasingly, and she couldn't help but stare at the fangs again. And then her attention lingered on his offered arm.

One of the terrible things about being a captive for ten years was she'd missed out on a decade's worth of living. Her mind was both innocent and rotten to the core. The men at the prison had done terrible things to her. She was no stranger to them. But she'd never been touched by a gentle hand, never had a relationship, and never had a chance for feelings to blossom for another person.

He saved our life, she accused herself in her head. *It's the only reason we feel this way.*

But her beast liked to disagree. *No, we likes him. We likes him lots.* She purred with a rattle, the gray and black patterns rolling across her skin. And now it was Warren's turn to watch *her* as the day settled into dusk, and her body could not help as it forced a partial transformation.

Her eyes flickered to yellow. Slick, black claws protruded from the ends of her fingertips. Fangs descended from her mouth, about twice as long as Warren's.

No more, she ordered her beast.

Yes more. We're safe here.

Her weakened body quickly lost the fight against her eager beast. Pain ripped at her shoulder blades, and she gritted her teeth as she braced herself against the wall. She glanced back and forth across the hallway to find somewhere to hide. But Warren unknowingly blocked her path.

The pattern on her skin slithered faster with anticipation just as black wings ripped from her back and unfurled on either side of her.

She gasped in both pain and relief like stretching an aching limb after so long of disuse. Somehow, she found the strength to fight back against her beast to prevent her entire transformation from unfurling.

Stop! she begged. *No more.*

The beast gave her a contented rattle and backed down. She wasn't ready to reveal her entire self to *anyone*. Especially not to Warren.

Self-consciousness led her to glance away and stare at the floor while she bashfully ran her hair through her fingers to give her anything to do than look his way.

Unexpectedly, Warren chuckled, and she couldn't help but lift her head to find amusement in his eyes. "So *this* is why you didn't like the dress I picked out. There's no room for your wings." He grinned from ear to ear, his pointed fangs more prominent than before. "I assumed you thought I had bad taste."

She grimaced and poked him in the chest. *You do have bad taste.*

He held his hands up in defense. "I thought you'd look pretty in it. But pretty is not what I would call you in this outfit."

She tipped her head to the side questioningly, all while a sliver of fear ran rampant through her mind. Did he think her ugly? Especially in this form?

But as his gaze raked down her body, she felt heat spark from his eyes as his attention lingered a little longer on the skin peeking out of her vest above her belt. At least until he blinked several times and tore his attention away from her.

He cleared his throat. "I like your wings. They suit you." And then he offered his arm again.

Wrap him up in coils, her beast sang inside her mind. *Take him as our mate.*

Stop! she mouthed, but then another round of embarrassment climbed her neck when she found Warren's attention fixed on her mouth, likely having seen her silent argument with her beast.

To try to hide her fluster, she took his arm. But it didn't help. Because now heat climbed her body for an entirely different reason. He was warm and safe, and being in his presence made her stomach turn and flip in the most pleasant way.

Rather than inquiring about her strange behavior, he began his promised tale. "There was once a group of people who lived high in the mountains, bred to be strong, fast, and resilient to men and nature. The emperor at the time ordered them to become his warriors. But their position was neutral. They fought for no one."

Kikka's grip tightened on his arm when she could guess what happened next.

He continued, "The emperor felt threatened by their existence and ordered his armies to hunt them down and kill them. Only a few survived."

She pointed to his chest, riveted by his tale.

But he shook his head. "No, not me. This happened hundreds of years ago. A few of them survived the attack, but they were scattered across the kingdoms."

All too quickly, they reached one of the back entrances to the mess hall. But she presumed people rarely used it, as no one bothered them in the shadows of the hallway.

Rather than escorting her through the door, he resumed his story. "Their descendants carried something called their *iskra*, or spark of magic, down their lines. And one day, a brave man decided to gather these descendants once more, those who demonstrated the spark no matter how potent or subdued." He gestured to himself. "They found me in a cold mountain pass, orphaned and alone as I begged for table scraps from the villagers. For eight years, I never had a name. I was called *that boy* or *brat* or *crumb cruncher*. And when the Umazi warriors found me, they gave me a name. Warren Steelsworn. They taught me how to wield the sword and how to harness my *iskra*. And when I passed the Umazi trials, they filed my canine teeth to sharp points and gifted me a silver sword."

Grabbing his hand, she pointed to his chest and then held up one of his fingers, mouthing *how many?*

He simply stared at her for a moment with furrowed brows until understanding seemed to pass over his eyes. "There are fifty of us in total so far. My friends and I, four of us, broke away from the group and started rescuing *others* like you."

Why? she asked, this time only with her enunciating the word with her mouth.

Although she was sure he couldn't have missed her meaning, he turned from her and acted as if he hadn't seen her question.

He opened the door and gestured to the dozens of tables filled with *others* like herself. Her mouth parted in awe to find two giant rock monsters in the corner of the room. A woman sitting at one of the tables by her lonesome sparkled like diamonds, her entire body almost translucent like glass.

She spotted shifters and saplings and everything in between. A half-man, half-bat hung from the ceiling as he munched on a piece of dried meat. Two men with pointed fangs and red eyes, likely vampires, argued back and forth at another table. And best of all? No one stared at her. No one batted an eye. Life was…normal here.

Warren released her and stepped away, not looking her way again. "Cyra is the fire-bird. Perhaps you can make friends with her."

Kikka spotted the woman in question burping a spark of flames from her mouth, recognizing her from the metal prison they'd been stuffed in together. She sighed in relief to find someone she knew, someone she thought she could trust.

She turned to thank Warren, but her heart fell when he was gone, no traces of him left behind except for the disappointment festering in her heart.

Before she managed to dwell on the feeling, the fire-bird grabbed onto her hand and pulled her toward their table, sitting her into a chair.

Kikka's heart momentarily burned with fear as she pulled herself in to become as small as possible. But it was difficult when her wings could only lay so flat.

"I insist you sit with us every day," Cyra said as she gestured to herself and her sapling friend, Aspen. "Enara will join us soon enough, I'm sure. She's feeling self-conscious about her plucked feathers."

Cyra's own feathers ruffled, a mesmerizing sheen of gold running across the beautiful orange and red pigments. Her legs were shaped like a human's but with rough skin like a bird, and then her feet grew outward with talons instead of toes. Feathers climbed across her arms and face, her wings attached at the arm. But her hands, lips, and eyes were more human than beast.

"You have wings," Aspen commented with awe as she reached out to touch the leathery membrane attached to Kikka's back. "All this time, I never knew. You never fully transformed."

She shook her head.

"I saw you with Warren." Cyra sighed. "I'm sorry he's so…prickly." Kikka shook her head again to protest, but Cyra held up a hand. "You already met me and my sister, Enara. Warren is like a brother to me." Her mouth turned downward into a frown. "There were once three of us. He fell in love with our sister who was killed by the hands of those who claimed to be monster hunters. They had planned to marry."

Oh.

Her beast ceased rolling across her skin as crushing disappointment filled both of them to the brim. Slowly, her wings receded from her back, her claws withdrew from her fingers, and her eyes transitioned back to green.

We are maimed, her beast lamented as it coiled into a tight ball inside her. *We are nothing.*

Oblivious to her hurt, Cyra said with a mouthful of stew, "He doesn't court anymore. After Astrid's death, he's never been the same. I wish he'd court. He's so serious and sad now. Someone like him deserves to be happy."

"There you are!" someone interrupted as they slumped into a chair beside her. She jumped, reaching for her knives. But then she relaxed, though only halfway, when she recognized Eldon, the wolf shifter, beside her. He handed her a bowl of stew, and unable to stop herself when she hadn't eaten in far too long, she quickly stuffed the food into her mouth.

"Kikka." He grinned at her surprise, hands resting behind his head. "Word travels fast around here. I heard it from my friend who heard it from his friend who overheard Warren and Gael mention that your name is Kikka."

We don't likes him, her beast bemoaned, shrinking farther into herself as if not giving the man the benefit of seeing this part of them.

We don't need a mate, Kikka reprimanded. *We are fine alone.*

Oh, but we have been waiting ages. And we don't likes this one. He sssmells wrong.

You are being melodramatic.

Yet, as she inhaled through her nose, she stiffened at the scent of sour dog. She tried not to grimace and instead tore off a chunk of bread and stuffed it into her mouth to try to disguise her disgust. She quickly lost herself in the hearty aroma and taste of her food. When was the last time she'd eaten so well?

She stiffened further when Eldon rested his arm on the back of her chair in a possessive manner. Her beast rattled threateningly, but the sound was drowned in the chaos of conversation around the mess hall.

The back of her neck prickled, her senses on high alert as she glanced over her shoulder.

Only to find Warren at the far end of the room watching them with a hard line set around his mouth.

She frowned and turned her attention back to her new friends. In a place so uncertain and foreign, she could use all the friends she could get.

And more than anything, she must forget about Warren Steelsworn entirely. The only path he led to was heartbreak.

CHAPTER *Four*

THE DAYS PASSED SLOWLY as Kikka's body healed from the injuries she'd sustained at the hands of her captors. The open, bleeding sores on her wrists scabbed over. Her knobby joints and bony limbs quickly filled out with meat and muscle when provided with good food and healthy sustenance. The shine in her hair returned after so long of being coated in dirt. After so many long years, she no longer feared her transformation. Although she wasn't ready to give into her full shift, she found herself able to relax when in half her serpent form.

And for the first time since her arrival at the fortress… She ventured outside.

The breath fled her lungs as she gazed up at grayish-orange clouds moving across a dark canvas above her. Flakes of snow drifted downward in a twirling dance, skipping and leaping and bowing to the whims of their freedom.

On the second story balcony, she approached the stone ledge and leaned precariously over the side as she caught a large flake in her hand. It quickly melted against the warmth of her skin. The joy of discovery coaxed a smile to her lips, and she laughed silently as she caught snowflake after snowflake, reveling in the pleasant chill they brought.

The flakes landed in her hair, on her eyelashes, brushed against her wings. Oh, the sky was so beautiful! Being chained up for years without seeing even a glimpse had been difficult.

But now that she was free?

The sky was hers to command.

At the thought, she attempted to spread her wings out on either side of her, wincing at the stiffness plaguing the leathery membrane. Her beast sang happily as she tried to lift them, tried to flap them. But years of disuse made them feel like something foreign jutting from her shoulder blades.

We fly! her beast exclaimed excitedly.

We flap, she corrected, clenching her jaw when working the muscles proved more difficult than she'd anticipated.

For years, she'd suppressed her beast. And this was one of the consequences.

After several minutes of straining against the bones in her wings, she finally managed to flap one side. But the other refused to cooperate, hanging nearly limp down her back.

"Your right side doesn't have the same muscular support as the left," someone commented behind her.

She gasped and spun around, startled to find Warren leaning against the door frame, watching her. The instinctual part of her wanted to throw her arms around him and hold him tight, basking in the safety he offered with his presence.

The other part of her wanted to shy away when he inspired feelings of attraction and infatuation.

"May I?" he asked. And after giving his request a pause, she finally nodded and turned around, facing her wings to him.

Her pulse raced as he approached. His gentle hand cupped beneath her wing, giving the support it needed for her to lift it higher. It was like an extra limb with the potential for her body to command, but after so long of disuse, it felt disconnected from the rest of her.

With his help, she managed to flap her wing several times, straining against the unused muscles in her back. But locating the muscles it needed to help her flap both wings proved difficult, especially after Warren released her. To fly again, she had to exercise those muscles daily. Multiple times a day.

"What did they do to you?" he murmured when she turned to face him. But then he grimaced. "You don't have to answer that." He grimaced again. "I am being rather insensitive. I'm sorry."

I wish I could speak to you. Her expression fell as she ran her fingers down her throat and next, lightly skimmed over his to try to convey her meaning. His throat bobbed with a swallow at her touch.

"Me too. But for what it's worth… You are quite good at conveying your thoughts as it is."

She bit her lip, one of her fangs narrowly avoiding pricking her. The simple action drew Warren's attention to her mouth. Though, was it a good stare or bad?

Likely curious, she decided, similar to how she'd stared at *his* fangs.

Taking a deep breath, she decided to confide in him. Because who else could she trust with her inner wounds? Cyra was her friend and roommate now. As well as Enara. But it wasn't quite the same. She trusted Warren. Felt safe with him body and soul. Dare she think it, she felt a special connection with him, one she couldn't quite explain.

She dragged her hand from her throat to her belly and then touched her wings while shaking her head. He stared at her, expression intense as if trying to figure out what she was trying to say.

"I assume you are confirming what I already suspected. They tried to cut out your beast."

An ache pounded in her heart as she recalled the long, torturous pain. The screams and blood and pleas for them to stop. At least until her voice no longer worked. She tried to push away the images, the pain. But like pulling open a curtain she'd long ago closed, she couldn't help but relive the horrifying situation all over again.

"Kikka?" Warren touched her shoulder, pulling her back to the present, only to realize heavy breaths heaved in and out of her lungs. He tried to pull her into an embrace, but she fought against him. As hard as it was, she needed him to know. She needed him to understand.

So, she dragged her hand down herself once more and then shook her head as she touched her wings.

Thankfully, he guessed correctly, not making her have to repeat living the most horrifying moment of her life. "They couldn't get your beast because you refused to shift." She nodded and finally allowed him to pull her into the safety of his chest. The strength of his arms surrounding her silently promised he would protect her from such mistreatment again.

"I can't imagine…" His voice caught. "I'm sure it must have been difficult to fight your shift."

She nodded again. Perhaps someday she might speak of it without inflicting pain on her soul. But she wanted at least one person to know.

She pulled away to give him the chance to see her face as she mouthed, *Thank you.*

For so much. For everything. For his comfort. For her rescue. For his kindness. For his listening ear.

But rather than replying, his gaze fixed on her eyes, and her heart nearly tumbled out of her chest when his attention dipped to her lips. He was so close. She couldn't move. Couldn't breathe. Her beast rattled excitedly, her skin changing patterns with growing anticipation.

But then her disappointment squeezed her chest tight when he dropped his arms, stepped backward, and averted his gaze. "Goodnight, Kikka."

And then he disappeared around the corner, back into the fortress, leaving her by her lonesome in the chilly winter atmosphere.

Notssss alone, her beast reminded her, giving her the comfort and strength she needed to push her disappointment away. Her beast, and albeit her, wanted Warren as a mate. But first…

She wanted to be as strong as she could be. To push herself to greater heights. To be worthy of herself, to feel pride for herself, to be someone all by herself.

By the end of the fortnight, she was going to fly.

And fly, she did.

CHAPTER *five*

THE NIGHT WAS QUIET.

Warren leaned against the cold stone wall of the parapet as he scanned the horizon for the hundredth time that night. Several deer passed through the snowy forests below. The lake they'd crossed over in the distance now lay shrouded in a layer of snow, but nothing passed over it. Not even the flash of wings from a nocturnal bird.

A quiet wind whispered through the surrounding area, picking up the snow from the ground and creating a chilling flurry. But otherwise, nothing overly concerning drew his attention.

Of course, he counted twelve nocturnal *others* outside the fortress, either hunting for game for their large group or wandering about on their own. But each would return before the dawn made its appearance.

A melancholy sigh escaped his mouth on his exhale as his shoulders slumped, his armor feeling heavy tonight. He liked taking the night watch. It allowed him to be alone with his thoughts. Away from other people.

But over the past few weeks, he'd felt...lonely.

As despairing emotions overcame him, he reached for the chain around his neck and grasped Astrid's feather in his hand. She had been gone for years now. His mind had already forgotten the details of her face, the sound of her voice, the strength of her presence.

If only he had been faster. Stronger. Smarter. If only she'd waited for him to escort her to the nearby town. If only she hadn't needed the escort in the first place.

He'd failed her. He no longer felt as if he deserved a place among his peers, afraid he might fail them, too.

Unwittingly, his thoughts turned to Kikka, reminding him exactly what happened when he *didn't* do his duty, when he allowed cruelty to happen by turning his back.

His fists clenched over the stone ledge, his jaw tight with emotion.

They'd only doubled their efforts to rescue this group of *others* when one of their own had been taken. When Enara had been the one in danger. While everyone else had suffered. Some for many years.

How could he have been so selfish? Kikka had suffered because he hadn't been there to help her, wrapped up in his own grief as he had been.

He had loved Astrid. But it was time to move on. It was time to let her go.

A heavy weight lifted off his shoulders, and he released a sigh of relief. The weight of her memory was astronomical. The burden of it was too heavy to carry. He was ready to move on. To move forward with his life. And perhaps he could start by taking more day shifts. Feeling a little less lonely wouldn't be a terrible thing.

The sound of heavy footsteps alerted him to his friend's approach as he climbed steep stone steps leading to the parapet. Gael's characteristic grin crested over the top of the landing.

"Are you on guard duty or falling asleep?" Gael asked, slapping his shoulder playfully.

Warren rolled his eyes. "I'm obviously doing my job. Can't say the same about you. You're twenty minutes late for your shift."

"I was busy."

"Doing what?" he huffed as he moved past him. But then he froze on the top stair as his friend answered.

"That snake girl has got everybody up in arms."

Warren spun around, brows furrowed as he instinctively reached for the pommel of his sword. "She's hurting people?"

Gael laughed and shook his head, taking a seat on a wooden bar stool after brushing the snow off its surface. "Oh yeah. Hurting lots of people. Breaking hearts, that is. That woman is gorgeous." He held a hand to his heart, a wounded expression on his face. "Alas, my advances were wholly unwelcome. She *hissed* at me."

Slowly, his worry melted into amusement, his hand dropping to his side. "Hissed at you? What did you do to the poor woman?"

"Nothing!" He threw his hands up in an exasperated manner. "All I said was she looked tempting and asked if she wanted to go somewhere quiet to talk."

"And you're surprised she denied you?" Warren wasn't sure why he felt a wave of relief at the discovery. "She doesn't like being alone with men."

His friend lifted an eyebrow and gave him a pointed stare. "She likes being alone with *you* plenty enough." He sighed dramatically. "It's a shame she can't actually speak." And then he waggled his eyebrows. "But you don't need a voice to put a pair of good lips to use."

Anger flooded through Warren's veins at the insinuation, and for a moment, he saw red. He smashed his foot into one of the legs of the stool Gael sat on. The other man cried out as the stool broke and dumped him onto the ground.

"Relax!" Gael gasped, holding up a begging hand. "I didn't mean it. I was only jesting."

Too worked up to form a reply that wasn't filled with scathing anger, Warren spun around and stamped down the stairs. Despite feeling exhausted only moments prior, rage lent him far more energy than he knew what to do with.

Rather than heading to his room to sleep, he stalked around the fortress toward the training grounds, muttering under his breath about his idiotic friend. The man managed to flirt with every new woman who came to the fortress, no matter what they looked like, as most of them were *others*. Usually, he didn't care. But he felt...*protective* over Kikka. Especially after everything she had gone through.

Over the past few weeks, he'd tried to keep his distance from her. But for whatever reason, the thought of her plagued his mind. And it didn't help finding out from Gael that she was a heart-breaking serpent. With wings.

The dim light of pre-dawn broke over the skies as he finally reached the outdoor training grounds. But he quickly realized…he wasn't alone.

A group of four shifters skirmished, two pitted against two, each with a sword in their hand. They moved on deft feet, striking and blocking with practiced maneuvers. He recognized them as the wolf shifters of the fortress. They were social with others but mainly kept to their own little group. One of them was mated to the female also skirmishing with them. The other two were single. Or at least, he thought so. He didn't tend to keep track of these things.

His heart gave a start when he spotted movement from the corner of his eye. Kikka watched the group fight amongst themselves from beside the straw dummies set up next to bales of hay. She used two daggers to copy the others' movements, slicing and stabbing and dodging, all while watching them closely.

Her efforts were admirable, but she shouldn't use sword techniques on dagger play. It didn't work quite the same.

Her movements ceased suddenly when she noticed his approach, and she watched him with caution in her eyes. He disliked the caution. Did she not trust him?

"Kikka," he said, suddenly finding himself breathless. The trip from the parapet to the training grounds must have winded him. And like last time, he couldn't help as his gaze slipped from her eyes and down the length of her body. She didn't dress like other women he knew. He loved how unique and utterly alluring she looked wearing fitted black pieces of leather. "Are you not cold?"

She didn't wear a cloak outside, showing off the moving black and gray patterns on her shoulders, collar bones, and lower stomach. The movement fascinated him, almost as if a snake slithered beneath her skin.

She shook her head at his question and pointed to her heart. Not for the first time, frustration vexed him from being unable to communicate well with her. He knew of only one way to hear her words through their thoughts, but bonding their souls using his *iskra* wasn't something he planned to do unless he was in a serious relationship, as it was the equivalent of marriage.

And, well, that wouldn't happen with anyone.

His attention shifted to the daggers in her hands, and for a moment, he cursed his own idiocy. Why had he never thought to arm her? She needed something to protect herself if the need arose.

"Would you like me to teach you?" he asked, nodding to her weapons.

A faint rattle reached his ears, coming from *within* her, though he had no idea from where. It almost sounded excited rather than threatened.

But when Kikka didn't reply immediately…

He swallowed when he realized she fixed her stare on the feather hanging around his neck, and he quickly shoved it beneath his shirt.

It doesn't matter if she sees it, he defended himself. *I'm not doing anything wrong.*

The feather wasn't to remember Astrid. But he kept it to remind him why he rescued *others*, why it was important to keep them safe.

"Well?" he reminded, giving her a playful nudge with his elbow.

She shook her head, turning around and approaching the shifters sparring on the field. They ceased their attacks, two of them turning toward her while the other two were clueless to her approach.

And then she tugged on Eldon's sleeve, and the man turned toward her. Their gazes locked, and a smile spread across his face and into his wolfy eyes.

She lifted the daggers and gave him a charming, sheepish smile.

Warren's grip tightened on the pommel of his sword until his knuckles turned white. Seeing them together irked him, and he hated watching as she shared her rare, delicate smile with him.

Using her expression alone, she silently asked him to teach her to use her weapons. And of course, the wolfy bastard agreed.

Warren turned away, unable to watch as he positioned her and taught her the basic strikes with a dagger. His anger quickly dissipated into dejection as he unsheathed his sword and practiced on the straw dummies, his back turned to them.

When Kikka had first arrived at the fortress, she had clung to him. And now? She pushed him away. Was it something he'd said? Had he done something to upset her?

The clean scent of freshly fallen snow entered his lungs with each labored breath as he parried with the unanimated dummy. Frustration continued to vex him, and with each passing moment, his movements quickened until his blade flashed with untamed velocity.

Kikka hissed.

He stumbled as the sound ripped him out of his intense concentration, and he barely managed to catch his footing rather than falling flat on his face in the snow. His gaze darted in her direction in time to witness her smacking Eldon's hand off her waist. Her fangs were bared, her eyes yellow.

"Don't be like that, sweets," Eldon said, which only elicited another hiss from her mouth. "We were having fun."

Eldon held onto the handle of her dagger, keeping it out of her reach as if trying to draw her closer. It was any wonder why she was breaking so many hearts when men were acting like arses. Women-starved men tended to be the pushiest of them all, taking things too far rather than reading the woman's cues to stop.

"Eldon," Warren said, his voice sharp and curt. "It's time for your border patrol."

"But—"

"You know how important it is to not be late."

The other man's lips pressed tightly together as his gaze darted from him to Kikka. After a few moments, he finally relinquished the blade and handed it back to her. With a gesture of his head, he motioned for the others in his small pack to join him outside the fortress gates for patrol. But before he left, he gave Kikka a not-so-subtle wink before shrinking down into his wolf form and trotting away from the training grounds.

The woman didn't betray her thoughts as she watched the man leave with no expression on her face, only her daggers clutched tightly in her hands.

"I'm sorry about him," Warren said as he sheathed his sword and swiped a strand of hair out of his face. "He's the alpha of the pack. He can be a bit much."

She pointed to his chest, silently asking a question with the shape of her brows. When her meaning was lost on him, she mouthed a single word he understood. *Alpha.*

"No, no, no. I'm not an alpha." Not even close, especially when he was far closer to human than *other*.

But then she pointed in the direction Eldon had disappeared, and relief relaxed his shoulders when he caught her meaning again.

"He only takes my orders because he has to. Not because he likes it. Those who don't contribute to the well-being of everyone in the fortress don't get to stay."

Her eyes snapped open as she pointed to herself and shook her head. Fear slithered rampant in her eyes, her mouth set with worry.

To appease her, he said, "Newcomers get a one-month grace period, as most are usually recovering from physical or mental wounds. You'll find something that suits you. If you want to stay."

She nodded her head, and this time, sheepishly held her daggers out to *him*.

Teach me? she mouthed.

He really should get to sleep. But he found he wasn't tired anymore. Especially as she ensnared him with the beautiful hue of her yellow eyes. He couldn't help but wonder if she could control the way her eyes changed color.

Finding a set of daggers for himself in the weapons cache near the fortress, he made sure not to touch her, not even to brush against her, as he first taught her how to maintain a defensive stance. When she seemed sturdy enough on her feet, he next instructed her how to dodge and block.

Defense came first. Always. Offense was trickier.

Kikka demonstrated several block maneuvers and then tried one of the offensive moves Eldon had taught her.

He grimaced, unable to hold it back when it was so very wrong. "Eldon is a good fighter." He switched his grip on his blade to Eldon's style of offense. "But he's much larger than you, and he taught you how to fight someone smaller." He changed grip again. "Fight like this. I doubt you will come across many opponents your size or smaller. They will likely be men. Taller. Stronger."

She did as he instructed and tried a swipe, clearly having never held a weapon in her life before her release from captivity. Her form was sloppy, which was to be expected. But more than anything, she lacked confidence.

"I'll show you what it should look like as you fight. What it should feel like." He bit his lip as he glanced her way. The vexing woman hissed at any man who drew too close. Would she hiss at him, too? "May I touch you?"

The familiar rattle sounded from her smaller form, louder than ever before. Her eyes flashed from yellow to green and back to yellow as if she fought an internal battle. The gray and black patterns rolled fast across her skin. Her fangs and nails lengthened.

But then the rattling softened, her body transitioning back to her most human form, including her green eyes.

She nodded. And rather than hissing as he placed his daggers aside and approached, she held her gaze steady, the intensity of it causing his pulse to flutter.

Slowly, he placed his hands on her slim shoulders and turned her around until her back was pressed against his chest. He wrapped his larger hands around hers where they held each dagger at the ready.

"Loosen your arms," he murmured in her ear. "Follow my footwork. Let me lead."

Together, they swiped at an invisible target, ducked beneath an imaginary blade, and stabbed upward to drive their dagger into the heart of the enemy. Kikka followed his footsteps, slow at first, and then she quickly fell into the pattern of side steps, turns, and leans as they parried and thrusted, blocked and dodged.

Their fight became a dance. Always moving. Never standing still. Together, they were one. One soul. One purpose. One blade.

They dispatched several more invisible enemies. After they stabbed their remaining foe and spun around, their rapid breaths escaped as foggy bursts. His heart trembled as she turned her head to meet his eye, her hair brushing against his shoulder.

Her green eyes were filled with excitement, with life. Her cheeks were flushed with an endearing rosy hue. Her hair was a beautiful, post-battle mess. And her lips… Pink and full and they curved into a smile. Just for him.

The breath shuddered from his lungs when all rational thought fled from him entirely. For a moment, he forgot about the vow he'd made to never pursue another romantic relationship. He forgot about how he'd wanted to distance himself from every woman who came his way. All he managed to focus on was the heat emanating from Kikka's body and seeping through his armor and into him. All he managed to notice were the quick breaths escaping from plump pink lips, the way the soft strands of her hair lay draped against his shoulder, the shape of her green eyes drawing him in and capturing his heart and soul.

The entire world disappeared around them, and for a few moments, only the two of them existed.

His *iskra* sparked within him, wanting to share a special connection with her and only her. And he almost gave into his inner desires. At least until he blinked several times, forcing himself out of his stupor.

Drat it all! He was no better than the touch-starved men vying for her attention at all hours of the day. He was supposed to be immune to such womanly charms. But with Kikka… It was different.

Because he realized…

Despite all his efforts to keep his distance, to stay away from the woman who managed to incite flutters in his belly and pleasant chills down his arms… He had grown feelings for her. Real, unexpected, romantic feelings.

Reluctantly, he dropped his hands to his sides and took a step backward, effectively halting his unforeseen desire in its tracks. His thoughts and emotions were jumbled, far too tangled for him to make sense of them. Not yet, at least.

He coughed into his hand and placed his focus on pulling the knot tighter where a leather cord attached his sword to his belt.

"Umm…" He chuckled nervously as he rubbed the back of his neck, giving her a sheepish smile. "We are in need of extra help in the greenhouse. I thought…" He coughed again. "If you were interested… I can show you…" Another cough. "I can give you a tour."

Internally, he rolled his eyes at himself. It had been years since he'd attempted to woo the opposite sex. And besides, he wasn't wooing her, exactly. He just wanted… Well, he wanted to spend more time with her.

Kikka nodded enthusiastically, which inspired another smile to lift on his lips.

"I have a little bit of down time tomorrow afternoon. Meet me then."

Rather than replying in her own little way, another excited rattle escaped her from within, giving away her feelings on the matter.

As he walked away with a smile on his face, he realized he looked forward to it just as much. He wanted to get to know the winged serpent a little more. And it helped if they found themselves someplace quiet to make the task easier.

CHAPTER Six

KISSSS HIM! Take him as our mate.

Hush! Kikka hissed at her beast as her hands flailed uselessly with overwhelming nervousness. She smoothed her hair. Fixed the lay of her vest. Took deep, calming breaths of humid air into her lungs.

The ceiling of the greenhouse towered over her, trapping the warm air inside rather than welcoming the flurries of an oncoming storm. Sunlight filtered through foggy glass. Vegetables and fruits of many varieties grew within fertile soil. Beautiful and colorful and a miracle considering the harsh weather blowing just outside.

When she was younger, she used to sneak seeds into the soil of her own family's greenhouse to find out if they would grow. Some of them would, but the gardener would quickly pluck them out once they became a small sapling, as he'd preferred order and neatness to the chaos of discovery.

She smiled at the memory as she ran her fingers through soft soil. Despite her parents' betrayal when they'd handed her over to cruel men, she managed to recall happy memories. Like the time she had raced through the meadow with her two older brothers and two younger sisters. The laughter they'd shared on a bright, sunny afternoon remained in her heart, even many years later.

She couldn't help but wonder where her siblings were now. What they were doing. Whether they were married or had someone special in their life.

A cold dread washed over the happy memories when she considered the possibility that one of them might have manifested a monster as well. With all her heart, she hoped not. No one deserved such terrible treatment. Especially not them.

Warm fingers touched her arm, startling her out of her rumination. Her mouth formed a silent scream despite nothing coming out. She instinctively twisted away but lost her footing, crashing to the ground with her back against one of the garden boxes.

With one hand, she flinched as she expected an oncoming attack, and with her other hand, she managed to draw her dagger from her belt and held it with a shaky hand between her and the threat, terrified breaths heaving from her lungs.

But it wasn't a threat standing over her with a shocked expression.

It was Warren.

Kikka dropped the dagger, and it fell to the ground in a clatter of metal. She buried her face inside her hands to hide her mortification at her instinctual reaction to a man's unexpected touch.

"Forgive me," Warren rasped, his voice closer as he knelt in front of her. "I wasn't thinking… It won't happen again. I swear it."

She shook her head, taking deep, calming breaths as she dropped her hands from her face.

It's not your fault, she wanted to say but didn't know how. *You just startled me.*

Instead of speaking the words she truly wanted to say when her voice wouldn't work, she lifted her hand and touched his cheek while shaking her head. *Hear me*, she begged, *even though I am silent. See me, even though I am a mystery to you. Touch me…*

Her thoughts trailed off, not daring to finish the sentence even in her mind. The beast within her desperately wanted a mate. To kiss and hold and warm themselves with someone else's heat. The need was instinctual, and she was unable to fight against it.

But…

Why would he choose her as a mate when she was maimed? When he clearly had someone else still weighing on his heart when the reminder of her dangled from his neck in the form of a yellow feather?

A shaky breath escaped her lips when she realized he'd moved closer, leaning into her, hovering above her. He captured her heart and soul with a single intense stare from his blue eyes burning with emotion. Though, she wasn't sure what emotion it was.

One of his hands braced against the ground while the other flirted with the hair brushing against her side.

Kissss, her beast rattled.

She wasn't sure if she moved closer or if he did when she felt his delightful heat emanating from his body and soaking into her like sunlight on a frosty morning.

"I will never hurt you," he promised in a husky tone as he grabbed her dagger from the ground and placed it into her hand, giving her fingers a squeeze. "You can trust me. Always."

I know.

Again, her beast rattled with desire as Warren's scent made her heady with longing, as his warm presence wrapped her up in safety, as his soft gaze dropped to her lips.

On the opposite end of the room, a chill wind entered the greenhouse as the door opened. Kikka and Warren scrambled away from each other when a hooded figure strode inside, his back hunched beneath his cloak, and black skin and long claws peeking out from beneath. He hardly spared them a glance as he made his way toward the back of the greenhouse and got to work.

Warren chuckled, rubbing the back of his neck as he offered a hand to help her to her feet. "I suppose I should show you around like I promised." He nodded toward the man in the cloak. "He's the main gardener and talks even less than you do." He chuckled again at his own jest, and she couldn't help but smile in response. "We call him Phantom. No one knows what he is nor what he can do. But he doesn't seem to mind the name."

Kikka glanced toward Phantom, watching as he quietly pruned the plants and trees on the opposite end of the greenhouse. Already, she felt a kinship with the man, as it was validating to meet someone who didn't or *couldn't* speak like her.

He led her around the humid room, showing her fruit trees, vegetable plants, and compost to make fertile soil. For someone who served the colony by using his *iskra* and sword to protect, he sure did know a lot about nature.

As if hearing her thoughts, he said, "When I was a boy, I worked with a lot of plants. Made myself useful by growing things to eat for my village."

She grinned as she recalled a happy time in her own childhood. She shrugged and mimicked climbing a tree and taking a bite of an apple. But he simply chuckled and moved on, not seeming to understand what she was trying to say.

He spoke only a little of his childhood spent as an orphan and told her stories about her time with the Umazi soldiers. He talked about his superiors and how they'd pushed him to do his best every day, training with magic and the sword until it became as natural as breathing. He spoke of his camaraderie with his peers, about how they were as close as brothers—and one sister.

As he talked about his life, she latched hungrily onto every word, wanting to know more about him. Who he was. Where he came from. What he wanted for his future.

But when she tried to speak of herself…

She tried not to become frustrated when he only understood half of what she said. More than anything, she wanted to speak to him. To divulge her thoughts, her feelings. But there was only so much she could act out.

"Warren," a voice said behind them, and they turned to find Koa dressed in armor, snowflakes dotting the strands of his blond hair tied back at the nape of his neck. The man's shoulders were rigid, the set of his grim eyebrows drawn together.

Immediately, Warren's expression became serious as well, his hand moving to rest on the pommel of his sword. "What happened?"

In a strained tone, Koa replied, "I don't know how, but the enemy managed to track us. They've been spotted across the lake." He looked him over and frowned. "You've been awake all night. Are you able to fight?"

He gripped the handle of his sword, his jaw set. Kikka clasped her hands to her heart when she realized he would have to leave her, to fight against the enemy who had tracked them. He could get hurt. He could die.

But still, he nodded. "Yes, I can fight."

They rounded up the soldiers one by one until only a third of them stood on the parapet, staying behind to protect those within the fortress. The rest of them gathered outside the fortress gates.

The way ahead was blocked by men and horses, weapons and armor, making it impossible to catch a glimpse of the one person Kikka wanted to see.

She spun around and found a distant, rickety wooden staircase leading to the top of the parapet. The unsteady structure wobbled as she placed one foot on the steps, followed by another.

Little by little, she climbed upward, swaying precariously with each foothold, until her head crested the top. She hugged one of the stone merlons and stared down at the soldiers below.

Her gaze swept across men—and a few women—adorned with weapons and armor, sitting on top of loyal steeds. The horses stamped their feet in anticipation of a battle about to ensue. She easily spotted Warren at the front of the group riding his own black destrier.

He looked magnificent. Born and bred for battle. His armor was sculpted to his physique, the weapons on his person right at home strapped to various places on his body.

She couldn't help but watch in awe as he turned his mount and rode back and forth across the front of the small army, shouting orders and reassurances like a true leader.

But then her awe turned sour as she recalled their very last interaction.

I want to come, she'd tried to say. *I can fight.*

"You would only be a liability." And then he'd turned away and hadn't looked back.

Of course, she wasn't foolish. She couldn't fight. Not well. Not in *this* form. But if he only saw how menacing her other form could be. How strong and powerful. She could fight. But he didn't want her there.

Blue eyes lifted from below and scanned the parapet…stopping on her. Warren held her gaze for several long moments, not glancing away as if trying to convey something to her. Perhaps it was a goodbye. Or maybe a warning to stay in the fortress. From this distance, she wasn't sure.

One thing she did know…her heart cracked when he finally glanced away to issue more orders.

Don't letsss him go, her beast hissed, rolling through her in agitation while only their tongue transformed and flicked out of their mouth with discontentment. *He's going to gets himssself killed.*

Warren is a strong warrior, she argued, fighting back against the tongue flicking but losing. *He will survive, and they will win the battle.*

No! Something isn't right. Something is very wrong.

What is it?

I don't know. I just don't know.

Over the years, she'd learned to never dismiss her beast's warnings. A decade ago, her beast had cautioned her against accompanying her parents into town. She hadn't listened. And there, she'd been captured and enslaved, willfully handed over to the enemy by those she'd trusted, by those she used to love. But not anymore. She refused to retain them in good light in her memories.

Her beast had good intuition, and if she sensed something was wrong. Perhaps she was right.

We can't let him go alone, she agreed.

But her beast pulled back reluctantly. *He doesn't want usss there.*

Kikka grinned as she stretched her wings out on either side of her, now much stronger and capable after exercising them every day. *I doubt he'll be watching the skies.*

Disappointment surged through Warren as he glanced up at the parapet once more, only to find that Kikka had disappeared. A part of him wished she had met him at the gate to say goodbye. But another part of him knew he didn't deserve her farewell.

He cursed himself for the curt words he'd said to her under stress. He hadn't meant to say she was a liability. What he had meant was he could never forgive himself if she got hurt and he couldn't protect her.

Now what was he to do?

Gaining her trust was no easy feat, and he feared he had lost it entirely.

I shouldn't care, he argued with himself as he turned his mount to face forward. *I should keep my distance*.

Yet, he *did* care, and he *didn't* want to stay away. She was beautiful and adorable, strong and courageous, even if she couldn't speak. He couldn't allow another man to swoop in and snatch her out of his weak grasp. He liked her. Maybe a bit too much. And he didn't want to share.

Focus, he reminded himself as he forced himself to pull his thoughts away from Kikka and concentrate on riding in the direction of the lake with their small army following behind. The enemy had brought fifty soldiers with them, stopping at the opposite edge of the frozen lake rather than crossing. Were they afraid to attempt to cross? Or were they waiting on something else?

"Remember!" Warren shouted as he turned his horse back around to deliver his speech. "They are not hostile. Yet. We will not attack unless they strike first. But our first priority is protecting those within the fortress. Under no circumstances are we to allow even a single one of them to breach our walls."

A single, "Hoorah!" lifted into the skies as the soldiers hyped themselves up for battle.

And with one last look over his small army of courageous Umazis and *others*, he turned his mount and kicked its flanks, leading them farther away from the fortress and toward an uncertain battlefield. Ice was not a good place to fight. Especially not with so many people and their horses on it at once. They were at a disadvantage. But then again, so was the enemy.

Clomping hooves and anxious snorts sounded behind him as he and Koa led the army at the front while continuously scanning the way ahead. Pine trees and snow stretched as far as the eye could see. At least until they broke through the trees and faced the frozen lake covered with a layer of snow.

Across the lake stood an army dressed in weapons and armor and riding mounts of their own. His stomach dipped uncomfortably when he recognized the king's black and yellow flag fluttering in a light breeze. From this distance, he couldn't tell if the king was with them, but he feared the worst if he was.

"Warren?" Koa murmured beside him, a silent question to his name.

If they battled against the king's own army, they would forever become outlaws in the kingdom, always looking over their shoulders, as they ran for a safer place.

"At ease," Warren replied as he dismounted on steady feet, ready to face what fate awaited him. "Our fortress is under no one's jurisdiction. Not even the king's."

"But we attacked his subjects in his lands."

"*I* attacked them," he corrected in a strong voice filled with certainty. "I acted alone."

"Don't do this. If we fall, we fall together."

He shook his head, trying to hide the way his hands shook by clutching onto the pommel of his sword. "There are too many to protect to take that chance. It's better for one to fall than for everyone to perish."

After a pause, his friend answered quietly, "What should we do if they turn hostile?"

He knew why Koa asked. Because should they become hostile, and Warren lost his life, Koa was second in command. The presence of the king's flag threatened everything they'd fought for over the years.

"Our priority hasn't changed. We need to protect our own, even if we must fight."

Without another word, nor another moment to consider the fear nipping at his cloak like the bitter wind brushing his exposed skin, he held his hand up with a clenched fist to signal to his people to stand down while he slowly advanced toward the enemy by his lonesome. A frosty gust of wind whipped through his hair, and he only wished he'd had the insight to tie it back to prevent it from fluttering in his face.

Anxiety rushed through his chest when a lone figure dressed in silver armor stepped forward, though he was quickly accompanied by two heavily armored men.

The four of them stopped near the center of the lake, several arm's widths between himself and the enemy.

Indeed, the king himself stared him down through cold, unflinching eyes, the man's deep scar running across his cheek giving away his identity. Apparently, the man had received the scar from one of the first *others* he'd enslaved. It was well-deserved, in his opinion.

The king spoke first. "You have attacked my men and stolen what is mine in *my* lands." He glanced toward the people a good distance behind Warren. "I was wondering where you were hiding them. You've led me straight to them."

"I've stolen nothing," Warren hissed, itching to reach for the sword tied to his belt but barely managing to restrain himself. "*Others* are not animals to be caged and tortured."

"Monsters," the man corrected, "are dangerous. I am doing my duty as King by protecting my people from such beasts."

"They are not any different from you and I."

But it was as if his words flew over the king's head as the man stroked his full red beard and watched him with calculating eyes. He gestured to the people behind him. "This is but a small portion of my army. If you don't give me what I want, I will hunt you all down with every sword loyal to the crown until not a single one of you remains."

His stomach churned with sickening dread as his gaze shifted over his shoulder to the waiting fortress tucked against the side of the mountain. These *others* relied on him for safety, for protection. He could handle a threat here and there. But fighting against the might of a king?

They would be slaughtered, with or without their *iskra*.

Turning back to the monarch, Warren couldn't contain his glare. "What do you want?"

"Ideally, I would want every monster you're hiding to serve under my rule. But…" The cunning glint in the man's eye seemed to grow larger by the second. "I will settle for your winged serpent."

Kikka.

"No!" Warren snarled, his *iskra* sparking between his fingertips as his need to protect her seemed to burn a hole straight through his chest. "Why her? Surely, you have other shifters who willingly fight for you."

The king took a single step forward, and in response, many of Warren's people drew their weapons, their swords and daggers singing from their sheaths in a unified, scraping rhythm. "Echidnas are rare creatures. They are strong. Resilient. Powerful. They can take down ten times more enemy soldiers than my average monster." A grin grew across his face, revealing one of the teeth cast in gold in his mouth. "We can cut her monster out and leave the rest of her behind for you to keep."

"Impossible," Warren rasped, his power growing angrier the longer the king spoke. "Separating the beast from its host will kill the host."

"Will it?"

He searched the man's face, trying to discern any lies hidden behind the smooth tongue of his. But he didn't find any deceit. At least none that was obvious. For all he knew, the king could have promised a pile of lifeless flesh after the deed was done.

But then the reality of the situation slammed him back into the present, to each cold, aching breath moving in and out of his lungs. To the tension in the air strung tighter than a bowstring about to snap. To the promise of war and bloodshed should he refuse the king's offer.

He recalled the terror in Kikka's eyes when he'd found her in the mobile prisons. Her frail, mutilated body. Whether or not it would kill her, cutting out her beast would cause her an extreme amount of pain. He could never allow such torture to happen again.

With a snarl on his face, Warren drew his sword. "I will kill every last one of your soldiers before I allow you to touch her."

The king's eyes grew cold and steely once more. "Then you have chosen a slaughter."

Wickedly fast, the other man swung his sword toward his head. Warren lifted his weapon to block the attack, but to his shock, the sword passed straight through him, making no contact at all.

The king and his guards weren't real. They were projections crafted from magic.

Before he managed to cry out a warning, a burst of magic slammed into him from across the lake. The momentum threw him off his feet, and he landed with a sickening thud on his back, his head cracking against the hard, thick ice.

His head swam with dizziness. His ears rang. Darkness seeped into the edges of his vision as he fought hard to remain conscious.

"Get off the ice!" Warren finally wheezed, his voice hardly loud enough for the others to hear his warning over their battle cries as they rushed forward to fight. He winced, his mind spinning as he tried but failed to pick himself off the ground, only managing to fall back onto his hands and knees.

His warning came too late. A thunderous boom shook the skies, followed by the faintest whistle growing louder somewhere above him. Through his hazy mind, he barely saw the small black speck arcing toward them, becoming larger with each passing moment.

"Retreat!" he shouted, managing to clamber to his feet for mere seconds before he slipped on the ice and crashed hard onto his side. "Retreat—"

The object flying through the air crashed into the ice, the weight and momentum of the large metal object shattering the ice beneath him. Deafening cracks drowned out the war cries as they transitioned into screams. Frigid water shot upward, grabbing onto his ankles and soaking his clothing.

Warren scrambled for a hold on the chunk of ice beneath him as it tipped precariously to one side, the chilly water threatening to drag him under. Behind him, numerous large cracks tried to strand them out on the water. Should any of them slip under the surface, the ice would trap them beneath and drown them if the chill of the water didn't kill them first.

He weakly climbed to his feet, gripping his sword in his hand as he fought to maintain his balance on the floating piece of ice. But then shock climbed his body when he spotted the single uncracked path leading to the safety of the lake's snowy shore. The air by the lakeside shimmered like a mirage during a hot day. Although he didn't know what it was, he managed to connect the pieces of the puzzle.

The king didn't want them dead when they were valuable assets to his army. He wanted to capture them.

There was only one way to escape. His people were headed straight into a trap.

He could do nothing other than watch as they sprinted toward safety, as one by one, they got caught in the mirage like flies entangled in a sticky spider web.

Warren retrieved his bow from over his shoulder and nocked an arrow. One way to stop someone's magic was to defeat it at its source. If he were to save his people, he needed to kill the caster.

A deep groan echoed beneath his feet as ice cracked like thunder rolling across the sky. A shaky exhale escaped his lips as he aimed his arrow toward the projection of the king's small army standing unmovingly across the lake.

The ice between his legs cracked straight down the middle, breaking slowly beneath his weight. But he stood his ground as he watched the army. Casting not one but *two* spells would cause someone to lose their concentration, to make a mistake.

Just as the ice split in half beneath him, he spotted the caster up ahead, the man's twitching fingers giving him away. Warren released his arrow a split second before the ice caved in beneath his feet, and then the lake's water swallowed him whole.

CHAPTER
Seven

NOTHING COULD PREPARE Kikka for the split second of terror of watching as the ice cracked under Warren's feet, as he disappeared beneath the lake. One moment, he stood on one of the broken ice caps, and in a single blink, he was gone.

A frozen wind whipped through her hair as she clumsily tipped her wings downward and dove toward the lake without a single thought for herself. Her heart pounded with panic, calling his name with every beat inside her chest.

Warren. Warren. Warren.

When he still didn't emerge from the depths of the lake, she angled her body between two ice caps and tucked her wings close before diving into the water headfirst after him.

The shock of the unbelievable chill washed over her, momentarily stunning her. For the space of ten heartbeats, she couldn't move, couldn't think, when the heat squeezed out of her body like the last embers of a fire.

Her beast thrashed within her, willing her to move, urging her to take action. She opened her eyes beneath the water, only to face darkness.

A new fear plagued her as she desperately searched the murky depths. Of never finding Warren, never seeing his face again, never hearing his laughter or witnessing his smile. Her heart ached at the thought of him disappearing from her life.

She couldn't allow it to happen.

Therefore, for the first time in ten years, she gave into her beast and allowed her transformation to wash over her, to change her, mold her, shape her. Her teeth and talons grew longer. Her wings stretched wider. Her legs came together to form a long, scaly serpent tail trailing behind her in the water.

The murkiness grew clearer with her full serpent eyes. The water became a plethora of tastes and sensations washing over her tongue. And her ears didn't only pick up muffled sounds as if they were clogged with cotton. She heard everything from slow, lazy fish moving their frozen fins at the bottom of the lake to shouts echoing above the surface of the water.

Her heart gave a start when she tasted something metallic on the tip of her forked tongue. Not blood but armor. Warren was close.

Her body darted quickly through the lake as she followed the metallic trail. Her lungs screamed for air as she dove deeper, deeper, deeper until she spotted him. Warren's eyes were closed, his long brown hair floating over his head as he sank beneath the weight of his armor.

Kikka lunged forward and wrapped her arms around his waist, trying in vain to propel them toward the surface. But his armor was too heavy.

Fingers flitting over the surface of the cold metal, she managed to unstrap one of his gauntlets, followed by the other. When his breastplate refused to budge, she instead used one of her sharp talons to slice through the metal until it broke free of his body and sank toward the bottom of the lake.

Again, she wrapped her arms around him as she tried to slither toward the surface, but another force fought against her—a strong current in the water pulling her in another direction.

She fought with all her might against the current, but it proved too strong even for her.

In a blinding, blurring motion, they were dragged through the water and toward the rocks jutting from the side of the lake beneath the water like underwater cliffs. She wrapped her arms protectively around Warren and squeezed her eyes shut as the rocks came at them blindingly fast.

And then they disappeared within a chasm and into the darkness unknown.

Warren's head broke the surface of the heavy, foreboding water that had threatened to drag him into their dark depths. He gasped and coughed and shivered as he tried to expel freezing water from his lungs. His entire body felt numb from his ears down to his toes. His head ached so fiercely that he was almost sure his body was going to combust.

He dragged himself out of the water and onto rough, damp rock, the absolute darkness surrounding him confusing his senses.

What happened?

He'd been dragged down by the water, his body unable to kick to the surface with the numbness spreading to all his limbs. And then something had grabbed him.

Panic raced through him when he attempted to stand, but his head smacked against a barrier of rock directly above him. There was only enough room to sit, and even then, the top of his wet hair brushed against the ceiling.

Terrifying blackness surrounded him, an utter darkness his human eyes couldn't penetrate. He didn't know where he was. He didn't know how to escape.

And the most horrifying realization?

He would not survive without warmth.

His body shivered uncontrollably. Each frozen breath escaped rapidly from tight lungs. Ice water soaked his hair and clothing. He reached for his *iskra* but it, too, seemed frozen, swirling languidly within his body as if it lacked the strength for him to draw it forth.

Something slick and wet slithered over his leg. He gasped and instinctively reached for a knife with stiff fingers, swiping it toward the monster.

A hiss echoed off the frozen cavern walls, followed by a threatening rattle as the beast moved away, distancing itself.

But then his eyes flashed open wide when he recognized the hiss.

"Kikka?" he gasped. "Forgive me. I'm so sorry!" He crawled on his hands and knees until he felt forward with his hands, his fingers grazing slick scales. "Did I injure you? What are you doing here?"

After a moment of stillness, of silence, the rattling continued across the rough floor of the cavern until the scales slithered over his foot and wrapped around his legs. The self-preserving part of him cried out in alarm as her tail continued to slither around him, tightening its grip until she held him at her mercy from his feet to his chest.

The more he struggled, the more her hold tightened. His panic escalated when the darkness also closed in on him, trapping him with no way out.

At least until a slim finger pressed against his lips and quieted the unease in his soul. Those same fingers brushed reassuringly through his hair and trailed from his temple to his cheek. A relieving heat emanated from her snake tail and wrapped him in a cocoon of warmth.

She wasn't trying to kill him. She was trying to save him.

Her talon tapped him against the chest. A question.

A frustrated sob escaped him when he didn't catch her meaning, when he couldn't see her face to understand what she might have asked. Now they would die together in absolute darkness with no way to communicate.

Although her grip on him loosened, allowing the air to better expand in his lungs, the heat she offered slowly melted the frigid iciness clinging to his body. His violent shivers eased into calmer trembles. His teeth ceased chattering. His fear of succumbing to a frosty death subsided.

And then a new dilemma hit him like a slap across the face. His *iskra* could be both calming and destructive. But it had its limits. And creating light from pitch black surroundings was one of them. He needed active heat to use as energy to form a light.

Currently, he had no such heat unless he stole what heat Kikka gave off. But then they would both be doomed, at the mercy of the cold atmosphere. Because if they were where he thought they were—in the winding caverns inside the mountain—he would be able to get them out of this maze only if he knew his surroundings.

Given the limitations of his *iskra* and the danger of their predicament, he could only think of one thing he had the power to do. One thing that might save them both.

And to do it, he must give up all hesitations of the future.

"I can't navigate this darkness without communicating with you." Distress leaked from his voice, and he blindly reached for her until his fingers brushed against her hand. It was clear she could see in the dark, her serpent eyes likely lending her the ability. "Will you allow me to bind our souls? It will allow you to hear my thoughts, and me yours."

She grabbed his hands and placed them on either side of her face before she furiously shook her head. Without seeing her expression, he wasn't sure what, exactly, her reservations were about the idea.

Still, he tried again. "I will only hear what you project to me. The rest will be private. I will likely feel some of your emotions as well." He swallowed, bracing himself for rejection. "I need your help."

He'd vowed to never form a relationship with anyone after Astrid, as losing someone was far too painful to bear. Asking this of her went far beyond the mere idea of a simple relationship. If they went through with this… It was as good as a marriage of convenience.

Or…perhaps more than just convenience, as his heart had other ideas than a platonic relationship. But he didn't dare speak those thoughts out loud.

However, this time she didn't shake her head as if wanting to learn more. She tapped his chest, a question he understood this time.

"It's a…marriage of souls. It can be undone. But it's not easy. Whatever we bind together today, it will be permanent. Unless we go through the difficult process of breaking it."

His teeth chattered as a sudden chill swept through him. He would not last long in this icy cavern. Rather than blindly stumbling around like disjointed fools, they could work together with their strengths to escape their prison of ice.

Despite the still, dark atmosphere, he felt the tension of her uncertainty pull tight between them. After a few moments, she gently pinched his ring finger. Another question.

A shaky breath escaped him, but then he winced when the action of simply breathing pained him. The fall through the ice had injured his ribs. "In my culture, binding souls is the equivalent of marriage." He gasped and winced when the freezing air numbed his lips and his lungs. He spoke faster. "But I don't want to corner you nor trap you. You have my word that I will never harm you, and the moment you say it's over, I will comply."

Kikka was a friend. He liked her, dare he think it, romantically. But it was still so new. And now he was offering nearly his entire self to her. For survival.

But he wasn't offering it casually. He meant to follow through. If she accepted him, then he planned to keep her. To provide for her. To care for her. To act as a spouse ought to.

A marriage of convenience. But with real commitment.

She loosened her tail's grip on him, and the moment she pulled away, a relentless chill shook him to the bones. He wanted to snatch her back, to borrow her heat. But he could not do so without losing whatever sliver of trust he'd gained thus far.

In the darkness, the slithering grew louder, followed by a rattle, until it ceased entirely. Taking its place was the quiet slap of wet shoes against ice, growing closer, until Kikka touched him again, gripping his forearms with her hands. He gripped her back. Desperate for her warmth. Needing to know she was all right.

"Is that a yes?"

A rattle. And then she squeezed his arms.

It was as good of a yes as he was going to get.

His teeth began chattering again, his limbs violently trembling. Desperation led his actions as he reached for his *iskra*. The power of it surged through his body when he couldn't find enough control to use only as much as he needed. It slammed into him like a relentless force, and he tried his best to grasp onto it rather than allow it to slip through his fingers.

"Bind us together, true as one," he said, his chattering teeth nearly making the words inaudible. "A love so great it cannot be undone." He grasped tighter onto Kikka's hands, fighting for consciousness when the intense chill threatened to drag him into further darkness. "Kikka, will you have me, Warren Steelsworn, as your loyal and loving bondmate, for now and until the end of time?"

She lifted his hands to her head to allow him to feel her nod.

Everything hurt so badly in his body, his tongue becoming numb just like his lips. But he forced himself to continue. "I promise to love you and cherish you and be by your side always. And so, I bind us together. Kikka and Warren. As one. One soul. One purpose. One bond."

Nothing held back, his *iskra* surged into both of them until every corner of his soul filled to the brim with the pressure of his power. He gasped and swayed where he sat on the frozen ground, clenching his teeth when the strength of the bond proved nearly too much to handle.

His ring finger burned as his *iskra* etched designs into his skin to make something that would resemble a tattoo in a circular shape around his finger. Like a ring but permanent. Kikka would receive one to match.

And then like a light snuffed out, his *iskra* faded completely, temporarily exhausted of its power.

It was done. He was bonded to Kikka in body, heart, and soul. She was his. And he was hers.

"Kikka." He struggled to reach for her slim shoulders with shaking, frozen fingers. "Can you feel the bond as I do?"

This time, she didn't reach for his hands to give her answer but responded in her mind instead. *Yes, I can feel it.*

He sighed in relief. "I've wanted to hear your voice for so long."

You can hear me. Kikka's voice inside his head trembled as if she didn't know whether to laugh or cry. *My world has been silent for so long.*

He couldn't help but smile at the soft quality of her voice. Gentle but with an underlying strength behind her words.

"Yes, I can hear you." And then he spoke to her through their minds, the sensation of sharing his intimate space with another person new and foreign. *And you can hear me.*

And then a second voice crashed into him, more forcefully than the last. *Wrap him up in coils! Take him as our—*

Shut it! Kikka warned.

"Ack!" he cried out loud. "There are two of you in there."

My beast, Kikka corrected.

Mmm, her beast said smoothly, almost as if it were caressing him with the length of its body. *We like this one lots. He smells delicious. Like grassy meadows in the springtime.*

We don't remember what spring smells like, Kikka argued with a hint of melancholy in her tone. *I'm so sorry, Warren. How could I possibly have told you she was a part of me?*

He blinked dazedly, trying to piece together the unexpected surprise. "Is this how it is for all shifters? Or just you?"

All of us. Or at least for the ones I've met. Some beasts are more involved than others. She's the only thing I've had for ten years, so she can be a bit loud.

"Ten?" he gasped. "You were locked up for ten years?"

Yes.

"How did you…" He cleared his throat when unexpected emotion caught like a brush snagging on knotted hair. His current physical discomforts shifted aside when all he wanted was to hear her voice, to get to know her better. "How did you get caught?"

I was never caught, she replied miserably. *My parents turned me in when I was eleven years old.*

"Your parents." He blinked slowly, trying to understand what cruelty could possibly stick to the hearts of someone who would willingly turn in their own daughter, knowing she would be tortured in captivity. "Kikka, I won't let anyone harm you again. I swear it."

He felt her overwhelming relief and gratitude slam into him moments before she threw her arms around his neck and held on tight, her face buried in his neck.

He embraced her around the waist, holding her close. For warmth. That was it. Nothing more.

At least, that's what he tried to tell himself even as a spark of joy lit in his heart like wet kindling catching fire. It was not meant to catch fire. It was meant to repel it. But he could not fight it.

And perhaps…he did not want to.

I'm sorry, Kikka said in a whispering voice in his head. Still, she held on as if she couldn't bring herself to release him. *I have not known kindness for a very long time.*

"Don't apologize," he murmured into her hair. "You can embrace me anytime you want."

His unexpected words froze him to the spot, surprising him with their fervency. There he was, accusing other men of being woman-starved, touch-starved. But he really was no better himself. Except for he planned to respect her and never force himself on her in any way.

To try to nudge them back onto the path of escape, he asked, "Can you see anything in here? It's pitch black for me."

She pulled away from him, but before she could retreat entirely, he snatched her hand and held it tight.

To not lose her in the darkness, of course.

It depends on whose eyes I use.

Her beast rattled and replied next, *I see ssssmall light.*

Kikka used their conjoined hands to point ahead of them. *We go this way. I don't think you'll survive trying to go back the way we came.*

"Why aren't you cold?" He cursed his chattering teeth as he followed her lead, each crawling on their hands and knees in the darkness. Somehow, they managed the feat while continuing to hold each other's hand. If even one of them were to slip and disappear, they both would. And he sure wasn't about to lose her to the icy caverns.

My beast keeps me warm.

Warm, warm, warm! her beast chanted, followed by a rattle. *We know lots of ways to keep him warm.*

Despite the misery running rampant through his body, Warren couldn't help but smirk at the beast's blatant innuendo and Kikka's rushed attempts to shush her.

After a minute of a numbing chill climbing his body as they crawled, Kikka soon guided him onto his feet when the cavern ceiling opened up over their heads. He still didn't know exactly where they were. How was he supposed to guide them out of the maze when his body wanted to collapse and never get back up?

Chills returned, his body shaking with unpleasant tremors as his teeth chattered and his limbs shivered. An intense fatigue weighed on his shoulders, and all he wanted was to sit down. To rest for a bit. But the more logical part of his brain knew that to stop moving meant to succumb to death.

You can't continue like this, Kikka's voice floated through his mind. *We have to find you warmth.*

When his lips became too numb to respond out loud, he replied in his mind, *It's not far, I'm sure. We can make it. We have to keep moving.* He squeezed his eyes shut when dizziness threatened to collapse him to his knees. *What do our surroundings look like?*

Like a cave.

He released a shuddering, shivering breath. *I need specifics.*

After a moment's pause, she explained in detail what their surroundings looked like, and when she described the steep drop-off to their left, he thought he had a vague idea where they were. He wasn't sure he could recall from memory how to escape the caverns without his sight, but it was all they had.

They only made it another few minutes before Kikka's intense fear crashed into him, followed by a hiss from her beast. Instinctually, he reached for his knife and held it between stiff fingers.

But nothing attacked them. Not even a scurry of small animal feet crossed their path.

"Kikka, what happened?" he asked, lips hardly obeying him as he tried to speak.

Her grip on his hand tightened, shivers now running through her body that seemed unrelated to the cold. *It's nothing. I'm fine.*

"You can tell me."

Another shiver followed a raspy breath. *These caverns only remind me of my time in captivity. They smell similar. They sound similar. I almost feel as if someone will jump out and grab me. Hurt me.*

He squeezed her hand, wishing he could offer her more comfort than a simple touch. And needing something to occupy his mind, to distract him from the agony racing through his body, he asked, "Do you want to talk about it?"

They traveled in silence down the length of another two corridors before she spoke again, her voice quiet through their shared connection. *When I was younger after first getting locked away, I'd managed to kill anyone who got too close with my venom. But after being starved and beaten for so long, I could no longer produce it.*

"Kikka…" he murmured.

She continued, *They most often came to me at night when my beast couldn't help but break free. I've suppressed my transformation for so long to keep from getting killed, but it didn't stop them from…*

Her beast rattled and hissed before saying, *They cuts us, we wants to cuts them.*

"How many times did they try?"

A few, Kikka whispered.

At the admission, her beast thrashed through their shared bond, rattling threateningly. *Blood. Pain! Next time, we will eats them. Next time!*

"There will never be a next time," Warren swore. "I promise on my life."

But then the dizziness in his head became too much to bear, and he collapsed first onto his hands and knees, and then onto his side. His promise was heartfelt, but he wasn't sure he could make it out of these caverns alive.

CHAPTER *Eight*

JUST HOLD ON! Kikka shouted in their minds.

Warren was hardly lucid as she grabbed him beneath the arms and dragged him toward one of the cavern walls to lean against the cool, rough surface.

Another chill raked down his spine when the rocky wall seeped its frigidness into his body. He suddenly felt tired enough to fall asleep, even with his wet clothing and frozen atmosphere. His eyelids drooped, but then he felt slender fingers cradle either side of his face before Kikka gently patted his cheek.

Stay awake. I will find a way to build a fire.

"You know how to build a fire?" he asked weakly.

Cyra taught me. Though, I'm not sure I'm very good at it.

His eyes drifted closed again as he heard Kikka's footsteps echo away from him and farther into the cavern. Sleep rolled into his mind like fog on a humid morning, overtaking him slowly until his mind could no longer fight against its influence.

Very slowly, his body ceased shaking, his mind whirring with flashes of images that he thought might be a dream but also suspected they were not. He recalled the faint flash of smoke. The rattle of a snake. Gentle hands touching his arms.

But then his eyelids cracked open to find Kikka bathed in a warm, orange glow. The flames of a fire flickered behind her and reflected off her long, wavy hair cascading over her shoulders. She knelt in front of him between his outstretched legs and helped ease him out of his sopping wet tunic.

Once again, shivers wracked down his frame when his bare skin made contact with the frozen cavern wall behind him.

You can't wear wet clothing, she explained as she laid the tunic out on the ground beside the fire. *You will be worse off wearing it.*

"Do you want me to take off my trousers, too?" he jested feebly, watching as adorable color climbed into her cheeks as she turned away from him, avoiding eye contact.

Whatever will keep you warm.

But he hadn't the strength to attempt the feat and tried to remain conscious as his body soaked in the heat from the flames. He glanced sluggishly around the cavern, recognizing the large crevice in one of the walls where Koa had once hidden in an attempt to scare them. Aiden had nearly jumped out of his skin at the time and had socked Koa in the face hard enough to give him a black eye.

His mouth twitched at the memory, at the hope of knowing they were close to an exit. Really close. But he wasn't sure he could stand on his own two feet to reach it when his body refused to move.

Kikka returned to her spot between his legs, hands resting in her lap as she whispered in her mind, *I can keep you warm. If you will allow it.*

An overwhelming desire to hold her in his arms struck him right through the chest. He wanted to hold her close, to breathe in her scent, to take what comfort and warmth she might offer him. But…

"The exit is just down this tunnel. We need to keep moving."

You can hardly move as it is, and I'm not sure I can carry you in this form.

His gaze passed over her, noting her lack of wings, talons, and tail. Beneath the dim light in the cavern, he thought her eyes were back to green. And her beast was strangely quiet as if sleeping.

"It's morning."

She nodded. *The earliest I can transform is dusk. And then my beast recedes to slumber at dawn. She's more tired than usual after our full transformation.*

He winced when the back of his head pressed against the wall, and only with his shirt off did he realize the stickiness he felt running down his neck wasn't water.

It was blood.

"I'm disappointed I never got to see your full transformation."

Another time, she promised.

Without another word, she crossed the remaining space between them on her hands and knees. She climbed onto his lap with her legs resting to one side of him while her arms wrapped around his neck. Her heat seeped into him, somehow warmer than the flames billowing behind her. Although her vest was still damp, the offered heat was far better than facing the chilly cavern without her.

Tell me about your people. Her voice was like a purr when spoken through her mind. It was alluring. Addictive. *The Umazi warriors. Do they care that you aren't with them now?*

He tried to shake his head, but his stiff neck refused to allow it. "We are meant to go our own way eventually, even if just for a short time. I trained and fought with them in our fortress in the mountains. They are like my siblings. Perhaps…perhaps one day you can meet all of them."

Although she didn't respond, she tightened her grip around his neck and held him closer.

His heart picked up a quick rhythm inside his chest at her proximity, at the sweet, tender way she held him. Her flowery scent filled his nostrils, wafting off the strands of her hair brushing against his jaw.

Perhaps he had never wanted to fall for someone again, but his heart couldn't help but want Kikka. It only took a disaster and a soul bond to make him realize the truth—he was already well on his way to falling for her, and he didn't want to stop it now.

The weakness in his body and his spinning mind pulled him back into the dark abyss of sleep, and this time, he couldn't bring himself to move nor wake when he became thoroughly lost in the darkness.

Kikka hadn't meant to fall asleep.

Which was why she shot upright in a panic to find the embers of the fire long gone out, a new unforgiving chill seeping through the rocks of the cavern and bathing them in miserably low temperatures.

Alarm shot through her when she found Warren still beneath her, his eyelashes covered in a layer of frost and his skin pale like snow. A metallic scent filled her nostrils, leading her to the trail of dried blood coursing over one of his shoulders.

Warren! she screamed in her mind as she shook his shoulders. But he didn't wake. If it weren't for the shallow breaths escaping his lips and the slow, languid beats of his heart, she would have thought him dead.

In a rush, she leaped to her feet, pulled his dry, discarded tunic over his stiff limbs, and desperately searched for anything she could use to carry him.

Farther down the tunnel nearer the exit, she found crates stacked against the cavern walls, each barred shut with nails. With all her might, she wrenched one of the lids off to find pieces of fabric soaked in alcohol and wooden branches to use for torches. In another, she found preserved jams and moldy bread as if someone had once planned to use these tunnels for an escape during an emergency.

Another crate held bundles of clothing. She snatched a black wool cloak and then proceeded to tie a rope around one side of a lid from a larger crate.

Rushing back toward Warren, she draped the cloak over the crate, heaved him on top, and wrapped the remaining cloak over his body to keep him warm.

Panic shuddered through her every breath as she heaved the sled forward and pulled him out of the cave and into a waiting blizzard. Had she known about the extra clothing and cloaks, this scenario might have been far different. But he'd been disoriented and confused at the time and hadn't mentioned them.

Desperation clung to her frosted breaths as she strained against Warren's weight as she tugged her hardest on the rope. The man's skin was pale, his lips turning blue. And no matter how hard she pulled, it wasn't fast enough.

Although her beast was tired, she was almost as panicked as she was. Together, they managed a partial transformation, even in the daytime. Her wings flapped almost uselessly as she tried to use their momentum to propel them forward through the snow. Every bump was like a mountain. Every obstacle in their path from stones to branches seemed like an impassable river.

Stay with me! she begged silently, but no matter how loud she screamed it in her mind, he remained unconscious, slowly freezing from the outside in.

She tugged and pulled until they rounded a bend in the trees, and only then did a silent sob of relief shake her frame. The fortress moved within sight, the imposing structure the only safe place she had ever known.

Spotting the fortress gave her the extra burst of energy she needed as she crested the top of a small hill. Careful to keep

Warren safe on the makeshift sled, she ran down the length of the other side of the hill, barely keeping ahead of the sled and steering it to avoid running into obstacles.

She wanted to scream. To shout for help. Not for the first time, she cursed her maimed throat, her lack of voice.

Heavy breaths escaped her lungs. Painful. Exhausted. Fatigued. But her discomfort paled in comparison to Warren's life. She would do anything to save him. Anything at all.

When she neared the fortress enough to spot several people on the parapet through the blizzard, she dropped the rope and waved her arms wildly, begging for help. A muffled shout reached her ears before one of them pointed to her location.

Another silent sob wracked her frame as she picked up the rope and pulled harder than ever before, fighting against her boots slipping over ice and snow. Every muscle in her body strained against the effort of propelling Warren forward rather than slipping backward when another small hill threatened to steal him away.

Just as she struggled over the hill, the sound of a gate screeching open preceded the pounding of a half-dozen horses galloping and snorting as their riders urged them forward at a brisk pace.

Kikka's legs collapsed beneath her just as the riders reached them. Two men lifted her onto a horse in front of Aiden, who held onto her with a tight grip as if afraid she might fall.

And then the others hefted Warren's limp, unconscious frame onto another horse with Koa before speeding back toward the fortress.

Is he alive? she tried to scream over the crashing wind in her ears. But no one heard her. Because she had no voice. All she could do was stare distressingly at his limp limbs and his head lolling to the side on Koa's shoulder.

She barely registered when they dismounted in front of the fortress, and also when Gael helped her inside the large doors, down a hallway, and into an expansive room filled with cots resting against the walls, some filled but most empty.

"Get him warm!" Koa shouted, and several people jumped into action. Aiden added logs to one of the two hearths closest to Warren's bed. They ridded him of his sodden clothing and changed him into a dry outfit. And then one by one, they piled blankets on top of him to trap warmth under the layers of fabric. One of the men also added a warming pan beneath the blankets near Warren's feet.

Kikka couldn't tear her gaze away as a white light shot out from Koa's hands and entered Warren's body. His *iskra*. Just like what Warren had used to bond their two souls together.

The coloring in Warren's face slowly became less pale after Koa's administration, but she couldn't even begin to relax when he was still unconscious.

"Sit down," Aiden ordered her as he pointed to a seat resting at the feet of a cot across the room.

She shook her head and pointed to Warren.

But then he frowned and gestured to her arm.

She inhaled sharply when she only just noticed the large amounts of blood gushing from a wound in her arm. This time, she sank into the chair and allowed Aiden to clean the wound.

Although she tried to remain stoic, she still winced and squeezed her eyes shut as he began stitching the wound closed.

When had she received it? When had—

Oh...

Warren had attacked her before he'd realized who she was. The wound was from his blade.

Aiden's fingers froze against her arm, and she opened her eyes in a panic to find out why he'd ceased his stitches. But he wasn't staring at Warren. His attention was fixed on her finger.

A black and white design hugged her ring finger, the colors weaving together to form an intricate pattern of points and swirls. It looked like a ring. But one that was tattooed on her finger.

"Warren bound himself to you." It wasn't a question but a statement.

She nodded.

Surprisingly, he chuckled wryly as he continued his stitching. "He'd better deserve you after the way you dove into the lake after him. Honestly, I could not see this match coming from a league away."

She tipped her head to the side. Asking a question. *Why?*

"Warren has not expressed interest in anyone for a long time. You must be special." He finished tying off the last stitch and bound the wound with a cloth to staunch the remaining bleeding. "There are many ways to communicate, Kikka. Not all *others* have voices. Perhaps you should learn sign language. Not all can hear, either. There are people here who can teach you. It might help."

Sign language...

Yes, it would most certainly help with communicating with others. But what about literacy? Did Warren know how to write? Could he teach her?

As her thoughts pulled back to him, she quickly rose from her chair and strode across the room, standing near the head of the bed and away from everyone as they attempted to revive Warren.

Little by little, his pale cheeks became flushed with color. His shivering ceased. His breaths evened out. But still, he did not wake.

Warren, she murmured in her mind as she located his limp hand beneath the blankets and gave his fingers a squeeze. *Can you hear me? I'm here. I won't leave you.*

She could almost swear she felt him squeeze back the faintest bit, but it might also have been her imagination.

Many pairs of eyes trailed her movements as she scooted up a chair and sat beside him, trying to give him whatever comfort she possibly could through her touch and silent voice alone. She dried his damp hair with a cloth and pressed her hands to his ears to try to warm them. Her eyebrows shot up when she found an earring pierced in one of his ears but not the other. But her attention quickly returned to the others fussing over him as they tried to keep him warm.

"He appears stable," Koa said, lifting Warren's eyelids to check his pupils. And then he shifted his gaze to her. "Warren saved us all by taking down that spellcaster. He allowed us to escape. What happened? How did you save him beneath the ice? When neither of you rose to the surface, we assumed the worst."

Her lips pressed together with frustration when she didn't know how to convey her story. She held one hand flat to represent ice, and her other hand whooshed beneath it.

"You swam underneath."

Her exhausted beast rattled with a similar frustration, patterns rolling across her skin before she coiled up to sleep. Kikka shook her head and tried acting it out again.

"You were sucked beneath."

Yes, she mouthed.

"Well, that's concerning." Koa turned away from her and spoke to the others, "Have him watched at all hours of the day and night. If there's any change, I want to be notified immediately."

Most of them left the room, aside from the few looking after him and the other people in the infirmary. But Kikka stayed. Because she could not fathom leaving his side for a single second when he was suffering.

And then...

All was quiet.

A woman she didn't recognize changed Warren's bed warmer. But otherwise, no one else bothered them aside from the periodic check-ins to make sure Warren was recovering.

Exhaustion lay heavy on her shoulders after both using her full shift as well as depleting every last bit of strength in her body. She wilted, no longer able to keep herself upright, and rested her head on Warren's shoulder.

She fought against her heavy eyelids as she recalled his words from the cavern, the words to bind their souls. *Bind us together, true as one. A love so great it cannot be undone.*

All her life, Kikka had never known what love truly was. Not after the people she had trusted the most had betrayed her in an unimaginable way. But this? As she thought of how sweetly and patiently Warren treated her, how he looked at her with such intensity as to melt her insides, she liked to think of it as love. As someone who cared about her, even if in such a capacity as friendship.

I promise to love you and cherish you and be by your side always. And so, I bind us together. Kikka and Warren. As one. One soul. One purpose. One bond.

A faint smile pulled up on her lips as her heavy lids won. Although she didn't know if Warren truly meant what he'd said, she knew she would treasure his words for the rest of her life.

CHAPTER *Nine*

HEAVY FOOTSTEPS ALERTED Kikka to someone's approach.

She shot upright into a sitting position, her eyes flashing yellow and her beast rattling threateningly as her instincts flailed. A familiar face stared at her accusingly from across the room, something between a glare and betrayal in his eyes.

"You *bonded* with him?" Eldon accused.

Even as he approached with furious footsteps, Kikka held her ground with her back straight and her hand slipping into Warren's where he still lay unconscious on the cot.

"I thought things were headed in a good direction between us. You couldn't even bother to *let me down gently?*"

She only wished she could speak to point out that she had never done anything to lead him on. Besides, the bond was still so new that even she didn't know where things were headed with Warren, nor if they would head anywhere at all.

Eldon gestured to all of Warren. "He's not the relationship kind of man. I could take care of you. Forget about him."

But she held tighter to Warren's limp hand and shook her head. He'd spoken vows to her, and she to him, if only in her mind. She would not betray him.

His nostrils flared before pointing an accusing finger at her throat. "He has the power to heal your voice. If he truly cares for you, why hasn't he done it?"

And then without another word, he spun on his heel and stormed out of the infirmary, leaving her staring after him in bewilderment.

Had he spoken the truth? Why would Warren bond himself to her if he could have healed her voice instead?

As she returned her gaze to Warren's sleeping face, she frowned. He owed her nothing. But if he didn't offer her voice to her, would she ever truly have his heart?

Sore. Stiff. Confused.

There had been only a handful of times in Warren's life when he'd woken in such circumstances, and this was one of them as he slowly blinked his eyes open to a vaguely familiar ceiling staring back at him.

Somewhere near him, a fire crackled, offering warmth when he otherwise felt a chill in his bones. He blinked several more times until his eyes adjusted on a waterfall of light brown hair cascading over a slender arm where it lay outstretched on a small table beside his cot.

Kikka.

He reached for her with a weak hand but let it drop back to his side as he decided to let her sleep. She looked beautiful as she slumbered. Her expression appeared relaxed, her long lashes casting a shadow over her cheekbones as she made an adorable sound from her nose. Like a snore but slightly more animalistic.

"She's been here all this time, you know."

He tipped his head to his opposite side to find Cyra sitting in another chair with knees tucked to her stomach, watching him closely with orange, blazing eyes.

"Where am I?" he croaked, his befuddled mind finding it difficult to make sense of the rows of beds in a large room and how he got there.

"The infirmary." She nodded toward Kikka. "She saved your life. Dragged your unconscious, frozen arse all the way home on a sled made of crates. And then she's been here for days, holding your hand and helping you get better." Cyra grinned. "She likes you quite a bit. And it seems you return her feelings."

His thoughts returned to the frozen cavern, back to how she'd protected him and aided him with escape. The memories near the end were hazy. But one thing he managed to recall was the determination in her green eyes, the passion.

"True…I like her." The word hardly did justice for the admiration he felt for her. "I like her a lot. She's sweet and charming and determined. Funny and brave."

Cyra laughed quietly as if to prevent Kikka from waking. "How do you know? She can't speak." But then her eyes widened with realization. "You bonded with her."

There was no use denying it. He nodded, wincing when the action pained his neck and chest. His entire body felt sore, and he took a moment to move all his fingers and toes, making sure everything was still intact and working. "It was out of necessity for survival. But our connection feels nice. I don't want it to end."

"You wouldn't have offered it if you didn't want it." She preened her arm feathers before she spoke again. "You must be serious about her."

"I am." It wasn't even a question. "But..." He released a long breath and glanced at Kikka once more. "I don't know if she truly wants this. I was...unkind to her before I left for battle. I'm surprised she went after me, risked her life to save mine." He swallowed. "Besides, I'm worried I'm moving too fast for her. She was a captive for a long time. I'm sure it's not easy to adjust to a life of freedom."

"She's been giving you doe eyes for weeks and you're surprised?" His friend laughed and smoothed back the orange feathers near her cheeks. "What's she like? Inside her head."

His gaze drifted to Kikka, and he couldn't help it as his eyes softened, as his heart burned with happiness. "Adorable but fierce. Brave and determined. The sound of her voice is rather pleasant."

Cyra smiled, but it held a hint of sadness to it. "You never bonded with Astrid. Kikka must be something special."

He swallowed. "She is."

Yes, he had cared for Astrid. But he'd been reluctant to create that bond. Perhaps this was why. Because he would share it with Kikka instead.

Of course, he could bond more than once, but it took a long time to break a single bond, as he had to travel back to his birthplace and have another Umazi warrior do it, one of his superiors. They did not look kindly on the divorcing of souls, even in death. But it was possible.

A part of him was relieved it was such a difficult process. Because he wanted to remain by Kikka's side. To find out how they could grow and blossom together.

"Favorably," Cyra continued, "if everyone knows you and Kikka are bonded, men will stop harassing her."

"She's being harassed?" Why, he oughta put these men in their places.

"Mostly by Eldon. He won't take no for an answer. Perhaps he'll finally leave her alone."

The sound of a rattle startled him, and his attention swerved in Kikka's direction to find her sitting upright, staring wide-eyed at him.

You're awake! she gasped inside his head. She rushed to his side and felt his forehead and then his neck. *I've been so worried. I thought for sure you wouldn't make it.*

"You doubt my strength?" he answered feebly, rather enjoying the way she fussed over him.

She wagged a finger at him. *I was warned the Umazi warriors were a little conceited. It seems as if they were right.*

Laughter escaped his mouth, but then he winced when the action pained his ribs. "Who told you that? Give me a name."

Cyra.

Warren attempted to glare at his friend on the opposite side of the bed but only found her smirking back at him, watching their interaction with amusement in her eyes. "Conceited, Cyra? Why would you say such a thing about me?" His lower lip jutted out in a mock pout as he held a wounded hand over his heart.

"Oh, hush now. You know it's a little bit true."

Kikka's gentle fingers took his chin and pulled his attention back to her. Oh, how he enjoyed even the smallest touch. And as he gazed back into her worried eyes, his attention drifting to her full, parted lips, he wished he could kiss her. But the time wasn't right.

You've been unconscious for days, her voice echoed quietly in his head. And then his heart melted entirely as she brushed her thumb along his cheek. *Don't ever do that to me again.*

"I can't make any promises."

She gave him a warning glare, and he chuckled.

"Fine, fine. I promise." Ignoring the weight of Cyra's stare, he asked, "Did you sustain any injuries? I'm struggling to recall some of the events."

Only one, she supplied hesitantly. *I'll be fine.*

"Show me."

After a moment's hesitation, she pulled down a bandage on her upper arm to reveal a gash pulled together by five stitches. His heart fell as he recalled when he'd attacked her thinking she was the enemy.

"I did that to you."

You didn't know it was me. I can't fault you for that.

"*I* fault myself for it. Please forgive me."

She sat on the edge of the bed and smoothed his hair back from his forehead. *There is nothing to forgive.* And then she smiled wryly. *Monsters are scary. How could you have known?*

This time, he answered silently as he caught onto her hand and gave it a squeeze. *You are not a monster. You are an* other. His brows furrowed. "Why is your beast quiet?"

We expended a lot of energy in our serpent form. She's tired.

"You must be exhausted as well."

She shrugged and gave him a half-smile. *How could I sleep soundly when I didn't know if you were going to recover?*

Emotion caught in his throat, making him unable to speak aloud. *Kikka…*

The sight of her soft smile held him captive, warming him from his toes to the roots of his hair. He had never wanted to enter another relationship until he'd met her. She was everything he never knew he wanted, everything he never knew he needed.

"As much as I enjoy a good one-sided conversation…" Cyra slapped her hands on her knees as she stood, effectively breaking the spell between them. "It's our turn to cook supper. Kikka, are you coming? Or would you like more time with Warren?"

Kikka tore her gaze away and brushed herself off as she joined Cyra. *How far does our bond reach?* she asked, looking anywhere but at him and even fiddling with one of her knives as if needing something for her hands to do.

I don't know. This is a first for me.

Her attention snapped back to him, surprise emanating from her wide eyes and open mouth. Clearly, she hadn't been expecting it, almost as if she'd thought he'd formed the bond with Astrid before her.

And then her mouth twitched with the faintest smile before she followed Cyra out of the infirmary.

Warren exhaled a long sigh, wincing at the discomfort of his sore muscles and weary bones. He tried to recall what had happened, what had brought him here, with more clarity than before. But hard as he tried, everything seemed like a hazy blur. He remembered Kikka keeping him warm. He even remembered falling through the ice.

He inhaled sharply as he recalled the king's trap. He pushed his blankets away with the attempt to stand, but his dizzy head forced him back into the pillows. He squeezed his eyes shut until his surroundings ceased spinning. As much as he wanted to get up, to get moving, he wasn't going anywhere.

Koa and Gael rushed into the infirmary, and the moment they spotted him awake, each of them grinned. Gael spoke first as he crossed the length of the room. "Good to see you made it through the worst of it."

"Have I?" Warren grunted, his head and body still aching fiercely from the ordeal. "What happened to the enemy?"

"There was only one man," Koa answered. "A spellcaster. After you felled him, we were able to get everyone back to the fortress safely."

"The king spoke to me. I think they were truly his words and not a projection." Panic raced through him again at the memory, and he couldn't help but reach out through his bond with Kikka like a gentle touch. In response, her warmth reached back, giving him the reassurance that she was alive and safe. "He wants Kikka back. I don't think…" A shudder ran down his spine as he considered their predicament. "Now that they know where we are, what's to stop them from attacking again but with a larger army this time? We have to flee. To move our people somewhere safer."

Koa ran a hand down his face and shook his head. "We can't do that. It's winter. Many of them won't survive the harsh cold."

A part of him knew that, but he couldn't risk Kikka's safety by staying. "Then we will remain and fight? There are two hundred of us and thousands of them. The king has *others*, too. It won't be a fight. It will be a slaughter."

Gael's *iskra* sparked between his fingertips in agitation. "How did they find us? We were careful about hiding our tracks."

Koa huffed. "We were hiding our tracks from humans. Not *others*. Someone might have followed our scent. Besides, even if we handed Kikka over, which we won't, how do we know the king would keep his word? How do we know they wouldn't slaughter us, anyway?"

A long, uneasy pause lingered in the room, filled with tension, dread, and worry. All the Umazi warriors at the fortress had vowed to rescue and shelter *others*. They'd all known it wasn't going to be easy. But their home had never been threatened before.

"You stay in bed," Gael finally ordered as he fingered the sword on his belt. "We'll inform the other soldiers about our predicament."

"Don't tell Kikka," Warren begged. "She's afraid of getting captured again, but I know she will turn herself over to keep everyone else safe."

Koa paused at the door, a frown on his face. "We're not going to let her get hurt. We promise you that."

Uneasiness continued to rake its claws down Warren's spine as the infirmary became eerily silent aside from the flames popping and crackling in the hearth. If the choice was to either fight or move everyone somewhere safer… What would give them the least amount of casualties?

"So?" Cyra playfully bumped Kikka with her hip as she cut up carrots and potatoes grown from the greenhouse. Each careful slice with the knife helped focus her mind, especially when it kept drifting back to Warren and the warmth of the bond connecting the two of them.

A part of her kept waiting for Warren to suggest they break the bond, especially when the reason they'd needed it was now gone. But the way he'd looked at her with such warmth and kindness in his eyes… The gentle way he'd touched her and spoken to her…

She didn't think he was going to try to break it. It gave her hope.

"Have you two kissed yet?" Cyra hissed in her ear as if to try to keep the other four from hearing their conversation. But each leaned closer, casting their gazes in their direction as if eager to hear the gossip.

Kikka smiled bashfully and shook her head.

"Do you want to?"

Rather than confirming it with a nod, she gave the fire-bird a pointed look. Who *wouldn't* want to kiss Warren Steelsworn? He was handsome and strong, brave and sure of himself.

Besides…she had never kissed anyone before. At least not of her own volition. And she couldn't just ask him for a kiss. That would be mortifying.

Her lips pressed together with uncertainty, her heart filled with self-conscious doubt. Their bond was one of convenience. She had no right to long for something more when their connection hadn't happened naturally. When it had happened too quickly.

"He likes you," Cyra sang under her breath, the side of her mouth stretching to the side in a smile. "But what is there not to like?"

So many things…

Her heart ached as she thought of her many shortcomings. Her scars. Her illiteracy. Her lack of skills in almost all areas of her life. What kind of mate could she possibly make when she didn't have much to offer in the first place?

She jumped, nearly dropping her knife, when Warren's voice sounded unexpectedly in her mind. *I never said thank you. For saving me. I wouldn't have survived without you.*

Warmth burned bright in her soul at simply conversing with him. This bond had opened a new door of communication for her, and she was grateful for it. *I apologize for not being able to save your armor. It's currently rusting away at the bottom of the lake.*

He chuckled through their shared bond. *It's any wonder you managed to get it off me in the first place.*

The fingers on the hand not wielding the knife flexed as she held herself back from extracting her claws. *I cut it off you. Therefore, it's likely not salvageable even if you do somehow manage to retrieve it.*

Remind me to never anger your beast. I don't think it's a fight I would win. He paused, the tap, tap, tap of her knife occupying her attention as she waited hopefully for more conversation. Through their connection, she felt a hesitant question on the tip of his tongue. *Does your beast have a name?*

As if hearing mention of herself, her beast stirred, rattling within her as she slithered and stretched. Of course, the first thing that came out of her mouth was a complaint. *We feelssss so old!*

She sighed and shook her head. *We're not that old.*

Even though she was twenty-one years old, she felt far older when she'd lived half her life in captivity. The things she'd seen… The things she'd experienced… They weighed on her soul. And she suspected they always would.

We are sssso old! Too old to not have a mate—

Panic crashed into her as she closed the door tight on her bond with Warren, essentially slamming it in his face, hoping against hope that he hadn't heard what her beast had said. Her heart raced. Heat climbed up her body and settled in her face. And for one horrifying moment, she could only stand still as mortification nailed her feet to the floor.

Allowing someone else into her mind, letting them share space with her and her beast was not something she'd ever anticipated having to do. Her beast was loud. A bit too honest. Voiced her opinions far too often. And now she worried she might scare Warren away.

She opened her door quickly to say, *She likes being called Beast. She does not understand the need for a name nor want one.* And then she slammed the door to their connection shut once more, breathing heavily with the anxiety of the potential damage her beast may have caused.

Cooking the rest of dinner passed quickly but also not quickly enough. Later, as she stood behind the table serving bowls of stew to everyone entering the mess hall, she craned her neck for a familiar face she longed to see.

However, Warren didn't make an appearance.

"Uh oh," Cyra murmured near her ear, her gaze flickering to Eldon who stalked toward them wearing a scowl. "Trouble ahead. Let's not allow Eldon to harass you again, hmm?" The fire-bird shoved a full bowl of stew in her hands and motioned with her head toward a side door. "Warren still needs to eat. Why don't you check on him?"

Before she had a chance to silently reply, Cyra pushed her toward the door and closed it behind her. Kikka let out a long, nervous breath as she gained enough courage to take the first step leading toward the infirmary, followed by another. As she traversed the loud, crowded hallways, she smoothed her hair and fixed her clothing.

However, as the day descended into dusk, a shudder ran through her body as her beast awakened fully. Her eyes flashed yellow. Her teeth elongated into sharp points. Her talons made it difficult to hold onto the bowl in her hands properly.

This time, she fought against the emergence of her wings as she peeked her head around the corner to peer into the infirmary. One of the feline-human healers quietly walked among the rows of beds, seeing to the patients. Six in all. She ventured that the others likely got injured when the ice broke across the lake's surface.

Her face pinched into a scowl when she noticed a steaming bowl of stew already in Warren's hands. Her beast rattled in agitation, though she managed to hold in a hiss. She didn't want anyone but herself to fuss over his well-being. She knew the possessiveness was unfounded. But she just couldn't help herself. Warren was *hers*.

She turned with the intention to return to the mess hall when Warren spoke in her mind. *You're not going anywhere. Come here.*

Bitttteee, her beast rattled excitedly. *Markkk. Claimmm.*

Stop it, she warned her beast as she met Warren's eye across the room. His coloring looked better, though he still lay back against his pillows as if he couldn't bring himself to get up.

Her worry reared its head as she crossed the room, set the extra bowl of stew aside, and peeked under the bandage on his head. A nasty bump still lay beneath, but it no longer bled.

She bit her lip, thinking of what Eldon had said about healing. *Can you heal yourself with your* iskra? *I thought I saw Koa healing you with his when you first arrived at the infirmary.*

Not wanting to betray her thoughts on the matter, she tried to keep her beast occupied by touching Warren. On the shoulder. The forehead. Checking him for a temperature. But other than his fatigue and head wound, he seemed fine.

Warren nodded slowly, wincing when the movement seemed to pain him. "Healing is very…consuming, for lack of a better word." As if absently, he lifted his hand and touched the base of her throat with the tip of his finger, trailing it down the scar to her collarbone. But then as if realizing what he was doing, he quickly dropped it. "Koa wasn't healing me. He was likely helping me get warm. We don't use our *iskra* to heal. None of us do, though we know how. Healing comes at the cost of ourselves. Of our own strength. Our own lifeforce. Healing something, sometimes even as little as a cut, has been known to kill an Umazi." He lifted his gaze to hers. "But I *can* do it."

Kikka angrily gnashed her teeth together, rattling with fury. Eldon had said Warren could heal her. He never mentioned that Warren could die from trying. She would rather never speak for the rest of her life than ask Warren to risk his life for her.

He tipped his head to the side, watching her. "I'm still trying to learn your rattles. Are you angry with me?"

She shook her head, not wanting to divulge her thoughts on the matter. For a moment, she'd gotten her hopes up. But magic couldn't simply cure the damage wrought by years of torture and captivity.

"I have something for you." With another wince, he reached toward the table and produced a book filled with hundreds of blank pages. However, the first few were covered with scribbles, letters she vaguely recognized from her childhood. "I would like to teach you how to read and write. If you are interested."

She nodded enthusiastically as she pulled up a chair and plopped down beside him. *Are you sure? Do you have the time for such a thing?*

"At the present moment?" He chuckled. "I do." He gave her hand a gentle squeeze. "Let's start with lesson number one."

CHAPTER
Ten

PRIDE BURST TO LIFE within Kikka like sparks of embers swirling and bouncing in the night sky. She finished writing the last flourish on parchment with a shaky hand, admiring the terrible scribbling job she'd created herself.

From where she sat on the floor in her shared room with her bunk mates, she held up her parchment for Cyra and Enara to see, smiling from ear to ear.

You are my friends, the parchment read. The words sounded juvenile and didn't do justice for how much she appreciated them. But Warren had spent hours upon hours teaching her how to form each letter and spell out the four simple words.

"Oh, how wonderful!" Cyra exclaimed, abandoning her laundry to embrace her around the neck. But she released her quickly when her feathers started to burn in her excitement. "You are one of the very best friends I've ever had."

Although still quiet and reclusive, even Enara smiled at the simple proclamation. Some of her black feathers had started to grow back around her face and arms, but she still often preferred to stay in their room rather than venture outside the door. Kikka didn't blame her. It had taken a while before she had felt brave enough to face the outside world herself.

"Warren taught you how to write that?" Cyra continued. Kikka nodded. "How long has he been in the infirmary?"

She held up six fingers.

"Six days?"

Another nod. Oh, how she wished to communicate better. But soon, she would be able to read and write, and perhaps even sign when she eventually learned that, too. Soon, she wouldn't be held back by her lack of voice.

Cyra tsked as she returned to her laundry and resumed folding her clothing. "Poor thing must be beside himself with boredom. He doesn't like to stay down for long. I bet he's itching to return to the training grounds with a sword in his hand."

"You're certainly right about that," a deep voice said from the doorway. Warren leaned casually against the door frame, arms crossed as his blue gaze honed in on Kikka. She startled upright, heart racing as she met his intense stare.

He gestured to her side of the room. "Pack your things. You're coming with me."

Cyra snickered across the room. Even Enara's mouth twitched as if they were in on a joke that went over her head.

She pressed a hand over her heart. *What have I done? Don't throw me out of the fortress. I'll work harder. I'll be useful. I promise.*

But he only rolled his eyes as he gestured with his head toward the hallway. "You are my soul bondmate. We're as good as married. It's not right for you to sleep away from me."

Slowly, her lips parted, and her stare nearly bore a hole through him. She realized she likely looked like a dimwit, but it couldn't be helped when he'd taken her completely off guard.

His soul bondmate?

She'd hardly dared to hope that their bond would be more than temporary. Had he actually meant the vows he'd spoken to her in the cave?

Unless you wish to break our bond? he asked in her mind. But she felt his reluctance through their pull to one another. It gave her hope.

Quickly, she shook her head and scrambled to pack what few belongings she owned. Her beast rattled excitedly, which only managed to flare her fluster hot in her face. Judging by several more snickers across the room, the others could hear it.

Wrap him up in coils, take him as our mate! her beast sang.

Stop! she hissed, not sure how it was possible for her face to heat any more than it already had. *He can probably hear you.*

However, Warren gave no indication that he'd heard what her beast had said, even when she faced him again with a single bag packed.

He promptly took the bag from her with one hand, and with the other, he intertwined his fingers with hers. It was then she decided she was wrong. Her face *could* grow even hotter.

Before they exited the room, Cyra called after them, "In the spring, we'll hold a real marriage ceremony with witnesses."

"We *had* a real ceremony," he argued, but she didn't miss the color rising to *his* ears this time.

"And we missed it," Cyra pouted. "Kikka deserves nothing less."

"All right, all right."

He tightened his grip on her hand and pulled her into the hallway. Although Warren set a brisk pace, difficult for her to match with her smaller strides, they still received stares from others in the fortress, as well as a few whistles and congratulations. Her *bondmate* clearly didn't like the attention, as she felt his discomfort growing with every step.

On the very opposite side of the fortress, they entered a quieter corridor with eight or so doors lining one side of the hallway, each with a symbol carved into the wood. The symbols were different from one another. Unique but conjoined in style and form.

Finally, they reached the door on the far right, and Warren released her hand to trace the symbol. "It says Steelsworn. The Umazi warriors have separate quarters from everyone else. It's…quieter here. When life gets chaotic…it helps to have somewhere I can enjoy a sliver of peace."

I like the chaos, she said as she, too, traced the symbol, staring at it curiously. *I got rather lonely in my cell.*

He dropped his hand to his side, and although she felt his gaze on her, she continued to study the symbol. "Would you prefer to stay in the room with Cyra and Enara?"

Do you want me to?

"Well, no. I spoke vows to you. And I would like the opportunity to keep them. But I don't want to deprive you of the chaos."

She shook her head and lifted her gaze, her stomach flipping pleasantly at the way his blue eyes ensnared her like hot vines wrapping around her heart. *There is chaos enough during the day. We're content with this.*

"We." He snorted before murmuring a foreign word under his breath, and in a flash of white light, the lock opened, and the door swung open leading to his—*their*—room. "I admit that will take some getting used to. There are two of you."

Well…yes and no. She took her bag from Warren and stepped foot inside the room, immediately awed by the racks housing dozens of weapons on the wall. A separate table held a plethora of armor, arranged in neat rows as if he had planned for her arrival and had organized all his belongings. *She is more like my inner self.*

Kikka turned in a full circle, fully aware of the moment Warren shut and locked the door behind them but needing something to occupy her attention rather than her pulse racing through her veins.

"So…I don't need to please both of you, make both happy."

Her hand roamed over the red and yellow woven blanket on top of the bed in the middle of the room, knitted in a beautiful autumn forest pattern.

She is easy to please. What makes me happy makes her happy.

Warren cleared his throat the moment she set her bag down on top of the bed. "Oh…I…well…" He cleared it again and gestured to a cot tucked against the wall on the opposite side of the room. "I thought you would sleep there. Unless you would rather trade. I…uh…didn't realize until now how much of an arse I was for making you sleep on the cot."

Her beast's excitement slowed to a crawl in tune with her falling heart. For once in many years, she felt the prickle of tears behind her eyes but quickly covered her wavering emotions with a smile as she crossed the room to the cot.

I am accustomed to sleeping on the ground. This will be preferable.

She reached for the blanket folded at the bottom of the cot, noting it was similar in design to the one on the larger bed. But the moment she held it in her arms, her tears gathered faster, hotter, quickly blurring her vision.

Why had Warren asked her to stay? Sharing a room with Cyra and Enara was far more appealing than the humiliation and rejection of sleeping in a corner of his room.

We are maimed! her beast cried, distraught over the situation. *Ugly! He doesn't want us. No one will!*

Warren froze on the opposite side of the room.

Kikka didn't turn toward him to seek what caused him to freeze, as her eyes pooled with moisture, and she wanted to hide her upset. What she wouldn't do to get her voice back, to be whole. Complete. Unmaimed. For most of her life, she'd known only cruelty and misery. Perhaps she'd been too hopeful. Perhaps she'd managed to trick herself into thinking that maybe she could be desirable to the right person.

She was right. She didn't need a mate. But oh, how her natural beastly instinct wanted one.

If only she wasn't cut up and scarred. Ugly. Maimed. If only she had the power to lift her voice for all to hear.

She swiped a hand beneath her nose when she struggled to keep her emotions at bay. Perhaps she should have declined the offer to sleep in his quarters. She was his bondmate, yes. But he likely wished she had feathers instead of scales. She could never compare to Astrid. The man still wore her feather around his neck.

Panic raced through her when Warren's footsteps pounded angrily toward her, and she could do nothing but freeze in place when her mind flashed back to hands grabbing her, smacking her, beating her.

But rather than cruel, rough hands, Warren touched her gently as he turned her around to face him, betraying the tears rolling down her cheeks. She hadn't cried in many years. Why now?

"Let me make one thing clear," he growled, slowly advancing until he backed her into the wall, the blanket in her arms acting as the only buffer between them. It wasn't fear pounding against her ribcage. Not even excitement. But something akin to anticipation. "I have desired you since the first day you arrived at the fortress. Your scars..."

She inhaled sharply when he dipped his head and grazed his lips against her throat. Her stomach dipped pleasantly. Her beast rattled excitedly.

"They are beautiful. *You* are beautiful." He kissed the scar leading between her collarbones. "Your scars show your bravery and your strength." He dipped down to one knee as his lips trailed farther over her clothing to just above her belly where the scar lay hidden beneath the fabric. "Your resilience and your courage. Do you know what everyone says about you?"

Tears fell from her eyes as she shook her head.

"They, especially the men, call you the heartbreaking serpent. How could you be ugly if so many seek out your attention?"

I thought some of my thoughts were supposed to be private.

He smirked. "Like you said, your beast is loud."

She is rather vocal, she agreed as she swiped at her cheeks.

His expression softened as he stood at his full height and brushed one of her errant tears away. "I am…terrified of making the wrong move. Of invading your space. Making you uncomfortable." He gestured to the cot. "I did not mean for this to have an adverse effect."

Still, she held tighter onto the blanket as she voiced her greatest insecurity. *Cyra told me about Astrid. How can you settle for me when you loved her so dearly? You keep a piece of her with you always.*

He took her hand and led her to his bed, gesturing for her to sit beside him. Then, he reached for the chain around his neck and pulled out the feather in question. A sad smile lifted on his lips as he unclasped the chain and held it up for her to see.

"I cared for Astrid. I feel responsible for her death. I could have done more. I should have prevented it. This feather…" He turned it around slowly until it fluttered gently in the air. "It represents *others* as a whole. It reminds me why I do what I do. What my purpose is in this life. And…" He set the feather and chain on the bedside table, his eyes twinkling mischievously. "Despite my best efforts, I've caught feelings for somebody else."

He ran a hand through his hair, giving her a side glance and an adorable half-smile.

Mmmm, her beast said, patterns slithering across her skin. Kikka's eyes flashed yellow. Her fangs descended from her mouth. Her nails lengthened. And then she gasped at the still-foreign feeling of wings ripping out of her back and stretching like a yawn. Night had fallen, sneaking up on her like a stealthy wildcat.

Her beast continued rolling across her skin, saying, *We do likes it when you kissss us.*

Kikka slapped herself in the face, shaking her head and squeezing her eyes shut as she fought off embarrassment. If she had the power to speak, she may have opted out of such a bond with Warren, as her beast was going to cause her a lot of unnecessary trouble.

Unexpectedly, Warren laughed. And in a smooth movement, he pinned her, wings and all, against the bed, a smile still stretching across his face. "I think I'm going to like this arrangement. It's much easier when your beast is so transparent."

Too transparent. Why was it that her own voice inside her mind could wobble with nerves?

"And tell me, Beast," he murmured huskily as he placed a kiss beneath her ear. Her entire body trembled with the ache of longing when his sweet, heated kisses trailed across her jaw. "Do you also like this?"

Both Kikka and her beast answered in unison, *Yesss.*

She gasped when his tongue traced the shell of her ear, but the breathy sound was quickly smothered by his kiss.

Her stomach twisted and pulled. Her heart fluttered. Every pore in her body heated with pure, unobstructed happiness until warm tears escaped the corners of her eyes and trailed down her face.

She had never been kissed before. Never touched by a warm, gentle hand. With just a single touch of his lips, Warren made her feel wanted. Desired. As if everything she lacked didn't matter, because she was enough.

His grip tightened on her pinned hands as he continued to kiss her. Softly. Sweetly. Until her tears dried and a shiver of desire trembled down her spine. She arched her back to bring herself closer to him. She inhaled his intoxicating scent driving her wild with every breath she took. Heat flashed in her body. The heat of wanting. The heat of desire. She wanted Warren as her mate. More than she wanted anything.

No longer able to keep her hands to herself, she freed them from where Warren had pinned them above her head and wrapped her arms around his neck, pulling him closer until not even a breath of space remained between them. Her long, clawed nails raked gently across his scalp, and he responded with a muffled groan against her lips.

Do you like this? she asked, her rattle sounding like a purr.

I think you already know the answer to that, he responded in her mind this time.

Just like when he'd guided her as they'd practiced fighting, their kisses became a dance of hearts and souls and fevered longing.

His lips broke away from her, and he trailed his tongue along her throat in lazy circles, over her collar bones, and down her torso as he undid her top one clasp at a time.

Halfway down, she caught his hands.

Yesss, her beast hissed.

No, Kikka replied more firmly.

Warren ceased his efforts and quickly dropped his hands. "If either one of you says no, I'm not going to push a boundary."

She wasn't sure why disappointment rained on her when he rolled off her, why her heart fell as he ceased touching her altogether. She wanted him to kiss her. To touch her. To take them as his mate. So why did she fight against her own self? Why had she stopped him?

Flashes of darkness seared her mind. Of cruel faces, rough hands, and deadly weapons. Pain, misery, and loneliness. But Warren wasn't any of those things. He was hope. He was freedom. He was love.

If she wanted him, then she must be brave.

In a fluid movement, Kikka rolled to the side, threw her leg over his waist, and straddled him, hands pinning his arms down similar to how he'd done it to her. The beastly part of herself couldn't help but flick her serpent tongue out at him in agitation. Or impatience. She wasn't sure.

His eyebrows shot up as he stared at her mouth. "What else can you do? You know, I still haven't actually seen you in your full serpent form."

Serpent later, she hissed, not sure if it was from her own mind or her serpent's. *Warren now.*

He burst into laughter, his chest heaving beneath her, but she quickly hushed the sound with a fervent kiss as her fingers reached for his shirt and began unfastening one button at a time. She waited for him to stop her.

He didn't.

Not even as her impatient fingers undid the last button and pushed his shirt open. Her hands ran over the muscles of his torso, strong and defined, every plane and groove a delightful discovery for her eager fingers.

Her long fingernails scratched him lightly from his chest to his stomach, not leaving a mark except for the sound of his groan imprinted in her mind forever. She cherished it and wanted to hear it again. For the rest of her life.

When he still didn't lift his hands to touch her as if still respecting the boundary she'd set, she snatched them where they lay on either side of him and guided them to her leathery wings.

A breathy sigh escaped her at the pleasant sensation of his fingers exploring every curve and fold of her wings. A rattling purr echoed within the room when he traced the pointed black tips at the top of the bone.

The rattling grew louder as he smoothed his hands down her curves, over her thighs, and cupped her from behind to pull her closer. The heat from their bodies pressed together elicited a burning sigh of pleasure from her lips.

She inhaled the scent of earthy, grassy meadows at his neck, and the heat wafting off his skin tempted her to bite. To mark him. To claim him as her own. She wasn't sure if she could produce venom anymore, but for her mate, and only for her mate, it would mark him as hers without hurting him, without killing him.

Her tongue traced the soft skin of his neck, her teeth gently nibbling him and bringing forth another sigh from his lips.

Let me bite you, she murmured in her mind, her talons digging into his shoulders without breaking the skin. *Let me mark you. Claim you as my mate.*

His soft gaze captured her heart and soul, never breaking eye contact as he kissed a trail of beautiful fire from her wrist to her palm, along each tip of her claws. "I trust you."

And then he tipped his head to the side in invitation.

Kikka could no longer hold back her natural urge to bite, and in a swift motion, she sank her serpent fangs into his neck. His gasp turned into moan as her venom escaped the tips of her fangs and entered his bloodstream. Should she have released her venom when threatened, it would have killed him. But when filled with overwhelming desire…

It was a different kind of venom. One he would thoroughly enjoy.

Another gasp of pleasure escaped him as he arched his back, bringing their bodies closer together. Until she finally unlatched her fangs when her beast was halfway sated after marking him as theirs.

She licked the twin droplets of blood trailing from the fang marks in his neck. Tasting him. Savoring him. Feeling their bond pull tighter now that she'd claimed him as her own. As her mate.

He was venom kissed.

Next, she guided his hands to her vest, wanting to pick up where they'd left off.

"Are you sure?" he asked huskily, his eyes hooded as he gazed up at her, clearly still dazed from the pleasant effect of her venom coursing through his blood.

Yes, I'm sure. She smoothed her fingers over the curves and ridges of his muscular chest, enjoying the sound of his heart picking up speed at her touch. *I want you as my mate. Fully. Unquestionably. Forever mine.*

"And you can have me," he whispered, digging his fingers into her hair and feathering soft kisses over her exposed shoulders. "A thousand times over."

And then Kikka threw caution out the window as she gave in fully to the heat of passion sparking between them, as they became mates in heart, body, and soul. Warren had been the one to rescue her. To pull her out of the darkness. To help her see her worth. He meant more to her than the entire world. And she hoped that someday, she might give him a fraction of the happiness that he offered her every single day.

CHAPTER *Eleven*

A SLEEPY SMILE lifted on Warren's lips in the darkness of early morning when a purring rattle shuddered against him, waking him from a light sleep. Kikka lay tucked into his side, her head resting against his shoulder as those adorable purr-rattles escaped her with every long exhale.

Just having her in his arms sparked another round of heat through his body, an unquenchable desire that couldn't seem to be put out like an eternal flame manifesting into being.

Wishing to make love to her for a fourth time that night, he ran his hand over her bare, slim shoulders, over the smooth membrane of her wings, but when he reached her hips, he froze his exploration when his fingers brushed against scales instead of skin.

Slowly, he lifted his head and caught the shimmer of scales against the pale light entering through the window. Rather than legs, a long, smooth tail slithered over the length of the bed, onto the floor, and wound about the room almost like tangled roots. At least until he spotted the very end of her tail when it rattled with lazy movement.

He had only ever seen Kikka in a partial transformation. In her full transformation…she was magnificent. Her wings stretched wider. Her tail was smooth and flawless. Her fangs were longer, and intimidating dark shadows rested around her eyes. But she didn't scare him. She wasn't a monster or just another *other*. She was the person who had managed to capture his frozen heart and warm it slowly, gently, in heated hands.

A second, hotter heat flushed through his body as he ran his hand over the back of her, over her smooth, beautiful scales. He didn't know how to make love to her in this form, but he most certainly wanted to learn.

But before he could try to wake her, a soft knock sounded on the door.

Warren frowned in confusion as he quietly climbed off the bed and pulled on a pair of trousers. Glancing back toward the bed at Kikka still sleeping, he opened the door to find Gael on the other side, distress evident on his face.

"What happened?" Warren murmured. "Is anyone hurt?"

Gael shook his head, though his attention drifted around Warren and to the coils of scales draped over the floors. The briefest knowing twitch of the other man's mouth was enough for Warren to push him backward into the hallway and shut the door behind him.

"You lucky dog!" Gael said quietly, punching him lightly in the shoulder. "Anyone else is fortunate if she doesn't hiss at them."

Rolling his eyes, Warren reminded, "Why are you here?"

Immediately, his friend's mouth pinched, and his expression tightened. "There are hundreds of soldiers headed our way. And this time, I don't think they're an illusion."

Warren swore under his breath and kicked the wall. But then he froze when he realized he didn't want to wake Kikka. This couldn't involve her. He needed to get her away from here. Far away. She was in danger.

Anxiety built up within him, and he pinched the bridge of his nose to ward off the coming ache. "What are we to do? We don't have the resources to prepare for a siege."

"Nor can we face the army. So many of ours will be killed."

Dread fell over him like a dark blanket as he recalled every face, every *other* depending on them for safety and protection. "There are children here. We'll have to get everyone out through the tunnels. We've prepared for this. I only wish it wouldn't have happened during the middle of winter."

Gael nodded in acknowledgement. Fleeing was their only option. "And what about Kikka?"

"What about her?" he growled. If the other man so much as suggested they hand over the woman he cared for, he would lose Warren, too.

He winced when he realized he couldn't abandon everyone else for Kikka. It went against every single vow he'd made as an Umazi warrior. But he couldn't abandon Kikka, either.

His friend leaned closer and lowered his voice. "She's the reason the king's army is marching on us. I'm worried we won't be able to protect everyone. To protect her." At the admonition, Warren's metaphorical hackles lowered. All of them had vowed to protect *others*. He was thankful Gael wouldn't back down on his vow. "The king has been stubborn thus far in trying to locate our people."

For the first time in many years, Warren witnessed uncertainty beneath Gael's usually confident demeanor. Doubt. Fear.

"We'll protect everyone," Warren promised, not sure he believed his own words. "We have to."

After a moment of hesitation, Gael's throat bobbed with a swallow before he nodded. "Get dressed. You'll want to see the army for yourself."

"And the *others*?"

"Cyra and Aspen are calmly waking them and instructing everyone to ready themselves for a cold journey. To prevent a widespread panic."

This isn't going to work…

But it had to.

"I'll meet you in the commons shortly. I'll need armor and weapons."

Just as he turned toward his room, Gael caught onto his arm. As if sensing his inner panic, he said, "We'll protect her. I promise. The king cannot have her."

When his reply lodged in his throat, he instead nodded his gratitude and continued through the bedroom door.

However, he stopped short when he found the bed empty and a cold breeze wafting through the open window. He gasped, sprinting across the room and shoving his head outside in search of Kikka. But he found nothing but fluttering snowflakes falling on top of the heads of their more capable warriors below as they gathered people and livestock for the long journey ahead.

Kikka was missing.

Heavy breaths filled his lungs. His head spun. Few thoughts clogged his mind but anxiety and panic. He moved backward, gasping again when he stepped on a crisp piece of parchment with juvenile handwriting. Next to it lay a single gray serpent scale half the size of his palm.

He stooped to pick the items up, and then his mind froze all over again when he read the single word written on the piece of parchment.

Sorry.

Somehow, Kikka had overheard their conversation. And as he had initially feared…

She was going to hand herself over to the king.

After weeks of becoming comfortable in her beast form, Kikka now felt naked as she braved chilly winds and flurries of snow in her human form. There were no comforting wings breaking free from her back. No elongated teeth nor tail to give her a burst of speed.

Although her beast rattled and slithered within her in agitation, she had never felt more alone. Especially after the wonderful night she had spent with her new mate in the safety and warmth of his embrace.

The fortress grew smaller and smaller behind her with every step she took forward, tracking the scents of beasts and armor and horses up ahead.

And the scent that used to be her home.

She blinked rapidly, trying her best to hold back warm tears as she caught two familiar scents that stood out from the rest. She recalled a warm lap, a tender embrace, and a gentle voice. She remembered the first time she'd ridden a horse, and the pride and happiness emanating from strong gray eyes.

And then the tender embrace had gone stiff and distant. The pride had turned into cold calculation when her beast had emerged.

Kikka's parents were here. She wished it would have been a happier reunion. But they'd betrayed her. Allowed men to torture and mutilate her. They were not her family. Just two people who shared her blood.

A shiver managed to worm its way through each of her limbs. Though, she wasn't sure if it stemmed from the cold or from fear. Because of overhearing Warren's and Gael's conversation, she now knew why the king was here. He wanted *her*. This was her fault. If she hadn't relied so heavily on the Umazis' protection, if she hadn't so desperately wanted a new home and people to call family, she might not have put everyone in danger.

Her beast wailed within her, trembling and thrashing and hissing. *We can'ts go back. We can'ts!*

With a trembling breath, Kikka halted in her tracks. *We have to. We have no choice.*

But yous will die! And I will be ensssslaved!

However, Kikka felt her beast's underlying fear. Not for herself, but for Kikka. For Warren. For being *alone*. Her beast did not want to live on her own. It was unnatural to cleave a shifter from its host.

Please, she whispered in her mind. *This isn't about us. Help me protect Warren.*

Her beast's thrashing calmed to an agitated slither before rolling into acceptance. Anger burned beneath her skin. Fury at what had been done to them, at what might happen to them again. But mostly fury at her parents. One way or another, they were going to answer for their misdeeds.

With her beast's acceptance, they continued forward. And as the encampment came into sight, horrifying flashes of memories burned holes through her skull. Long knives. Rough hands. Bleeding wounds. Pain. Misery. Despair.

She clenched her fists at her side and snarled. She'd only just found her freedom. If she must fight to keep it, then so be it.

One of their scouts noticed her first, riding out on a snowy path to meet her. Surely, he'd thought she was a damsel in distress. She was a woman with no coat, no protection, and she was by her lonesome.

But upon seeing her, the man gasped, stopping his horse several paces away. "Y-y-you…" He blinked several times, shaking his head before glancing back toward the camp. "I know who you are. You're dead." He seemed to know *who* she was but not *what* she was.

Unable to say anything, she shook her head, trying not to dwell on what it meant to be unable to communicate. This was not going to go well.

The man took off his own cloak and offered it to her. But she shook her head again. She needed her back unobstructed for her wings should she need to fight.

He hopped down from his horse and offered that to her instead. For a moment, she contemplated climbing up and riding far, far away from here. To escape. To find freedom. But she would sooner get thrown from the creature than ride to safety when she had only ridden a handful of times in her life.

Again, she shook her head.

The man led her back toward the camp, and by the time they arrived, a wall of soldiers stood between her and the real enemy. But after laying their eyes on her, seeming to recognize who she was, the soldiers shifted uncomfortably from foot to foot, glancing at each other and then back at her while hushed whispers lifted into the cold, gray skies. Some of them lowered their weapons. Others glanced with confusion at something behind them.

Come out and face me yourselves! she screamed in her mind, only wishing to project her voice from her throat and through her lips. But she still could not speak, only rattle threateningly, enough for the soldier beside her to take an uncertain step backward.

"I'm surprised!" a deep voice boomed from behind the soldiers, loud enough to hear over the tense breeze and whispered words of confusion. The soldiers parted to allow a single man through, one adorned in steel boots and metal armor. Kikka's breath caught in terror at the familiar cold, calculating gray eyes staring back at her and the red-brown beard covering his face. Though, after ten years, his hair was now speckled with gray. "You came alone. I'm almost disappointed it was so easy."

Two other men joined his side, and it felt as if her stomach tumbled down a flight of stairs when she recognized their faces. The princes. Much older. But the same eyes, the same hair, and uncertain expressions as they glanced between her and their father.

The older prince's mouth fell open, Jon, and she heard his breath catch. "Kikka? But…but…"

"She's not alone." Warren's familiar voice caressed her soul as he appeared seemingly out of thin air in a spark of silver. Behind him, Gael, Aiden, and Koa also appeared, silver sparking between their fingers as if readying themselves for a fight.

Her throat clogged with emotion when her gaze darted to the necklace Warren wore blatantly around his neck. It contained Astrid's familiar yellow feather. But also, her serpent scale now as well. It was almost like a declaration of his feelings for her, like dedication and loyalty. It meant more to her than he could possibly realize.

Why did you come? she cried in her mind. *He will kill you!*

You underestimate us. He shifted his endearing gaze to her for a mere moment before staring down the enemy. *We can handle this threat.*

Kikka wasn't so sure they could. Not with only five of them to fight against an entire army. Who knew how many *others* they would also battle against?

The king laughed, shaking his head as if unintimidated by the danger they posed. "If I were you, I would think twice about raising a sword to strike against my army. If you hurt us, you hurt your precious echidna." The man held out his hand, and once again, the soldiers parted to allow another figure through, this one smaller and slighter.

Tears threatened to fall as she stared back at green eyes, long, wavy brown hair, and a familiar face with a few more wrinkles and aging spots than she remembered. Had Kikka been twenty years older, she might have found herself staring back into a mirror.

Warren inhaled sharply as he glanced between the two of them, making the connection. "You're the king's *daughter?*" *Why didn't you tell me?*

Concern and anger flashed through their bond, but she wasn't sure if it was directed at her or her parents.

Because parents don't throw their children away for their own selfish desires. She lifted her chin and stared back at her bondmate. *Because the moment they betrayed me, the moment they handed me over to captivity, I no longer considered them family. I don't want to be associated with them. They broke my heart.*

"My first daughter," the king confirmed with a nod, glancing warily at the soldiers stationed around them. "She was sent away to the countryside because of her ailment. I know some thought her dead. But she is very much alive."

Ailment? Kikka screeched, her beast growing stronger, bolder as she thrashed against her constraints. *You tried to kill me to have a beast fight for your army!*

Her parents seemed confused why she didn't speak, but thankfully, Warren repeated her words out loud.

Her mother shook her head sadly. "You misunderstood our intentions. We sought to sever your beast from your body. The echidna would fight in our army. And you… You would finally come home."

You wretches! she screamed again as fury pulsed through her blood. *It would have killed me. I would have died.*

Warren repeated her words. The king's nostrils flared, his eyes flashing dangerously. "You should be grateful we didn't banish you entirely! Or worse. We gave you a chance. You could have submitted to the blade. But you refused to cooperate."

She dragged her finger from her throat to her navel. *Look what they did to me. Would you have submitted under such circumstances?*

After Warren relayed her message, the queen spun on the king and frowned. "You promised me they wouldn't harm her throat. Our daughter can't even speak to us."

"Severing beast from host is not always easy. Sometimes sacrifices must be made."

Emotional fatigue pressed heavy on her shoulders upon facing the two people who had made her want to die a hundred deaths to escape her torture and captivity. *You locked me up for ten years. Not so much as a single visit. You betrayed me. Don't pretend you ever wanted me back.*

She held out her wrists to show the multitude of scars from her chains. She angled her chin to better display the damage at her throat. Her scars went far deeper than mere flesh wounds. But it was impossible to convey the pain and misery they had inflicted upon her.

Again, the queen hissed to her husband, "You promised she was comfortable."

"It doesn't matter!" he thundered, banging a metal glove against his armored chest. "I wanted her echidna. Her comfort did not matter to me."

"You could have killed our child!"

"We have other children! Useful *male* children. Losing one, a girl, for the sake of the rest is sometimes the sacrifice we must make."

Fury burned behind Kikka's eyes. The pain of betrayal. The hurt of rejection. Loss. So much loss. They'd stolen her freedom, her autonomy, ten years of her life! And all for what? Because her father had wanted a powerful monster to fight in his wars?

He was greedy. Selfish. Thought of no one but himself.

Her claws shot out from her fingertips. Her elongated teeth snapped downward.

"Kikka, no!" Warren shouted.

But she couldn't stop her transformation now. Not when her beast had a mind and fury of its own. Wings shot outward from her back. Her eyes flashed a dangerous yellow. Her legs melded together to form a long, sturdy tail covered in tough scales.

Rather than screaming and running for his life like many of the soldiers did, the king laughed, his eyes gleaming with wicked excitement. "Finally! There are other ways to separate beast from host when transformed. Soldiers! Shoot her with the poisoned arrows."

"No!" the queen screamed as she jumped on the king's back, trying to choke him from behind. But he was stronger than her and managed to fling her off him. She crashed into the snow and tried to scramble back to her feet, but a soldier held her firm from behind.

Witnessing her mother trying to protect her, even after everything that had happened, sparked a newfound desperation to keep her safe. Perhaps what had been done hadn't been right. But her mother was on her side.

When the rage burning deep inside her reached its peak, she couldn't help but lunge forward and attack.

CHAPTER
Twelve

IN ONE SWOOP of her powerful tail, Kikka sent a line of soldiers flying backward before they crashed into heaps of weapons and armor. The soldiers out of immediate range of Kikka drew back their arrows, took aim, and released their poison.

Warren reacted quickly, delving deep into his *iskra* and erecting a translucent, silver barrier in front of her. Dozens of arrows hit the surface, sparking small flames, until each arrow burned to a crisp, its ashes scattering with the wind.

True terror snapped inside him as he realized the amount of danger Kikka was in. How many soldiers could they fight off before one of the arrows managed to nick her? From how it sounded, her beast would live. But Kikka?

She would not.

"Stand down!" the older prince, Jon, shrieked over the clamor of weapons, armor, and deafening echidna screeches as he ducked beneath Kikka's tail. "Soldiers, stand down!"

Half the soldiers lowered their weapons in confusion. The other half continued to fire their arrows. Kikka lunged toward the ones still fighting, and with only two swipes of her claws, she took out two more soldiers.

Warren and Koa used their *iskra* to create a concentrated blast to hit as many soldiers as possible, even if the control was sloppy. White light crashed into the enemy, clearing another two paths. At least until more soldiers filled the gaps, some of them monsters fighting for the enemy.

Prince Jon drew his sword and dispatched the soldier holding his mother in a choke hold. The queen gasped for air while scrambling toward Kikka to stand protectively in front of her, even without a weapon to aid her. She was like a mama bear protecting her cub despite her cub not needing protection.

When Jon and his younger brother, Oskar, now stood in front of Kikka with swords drawn, more of the soldiers ceased fighting in their confusion.

"You are making a grave mistake!" the king thundered, stalking forward with his own weapon held at the ready. "Move, Jon! Or I will be forced to cut you down for defying me."

Sweat dripped down Warren's face as he tried with all his might to keep the *iskra* barrier in front of Kikka erect. If it dropped, one of those poisoned arrows would surely hit her.

"You've led me to believe Kikka was sick!" Jon shouted back over the singing of metallic armor and weapons in the background. "You never told me she was a shifter!" The prince tightened his grip on his weapon, and Warren moved to stand closer to him to fight by his side if necessary. "You never mentioned that you cut her up. *Mutilated* her! She's my sister!"

The king's face stretched into a menacing snarl moments before he swung his sword at his heir, at his own kin. Jon blocked the blow and delivered one of his own, and the two parried back and forth in a fight not just to spar, but to kill. To protect. To claim.

Warren didn't dare raise his hand against the king. It would forever bring vengeance upon his people. But he would if he must.

One of the soldiers still fighting charged at Kikka when her back was turned as she fought against several *others*. Warren shot another blast of *iskra* toward the man. It hit him squarely in the chest and sent him flying backward until he crashed into the snow in a heap of armor and tangled limbs.

He spun around just in time to witness the king disarming Jon after a few expert maneuvers. Time seemed to slow as the king drew back his weapon with the intent to deliver on his promise to cut Jon down.

Warren rushed forward, but he wasn't fast enough.

However, Kikka *was*.

She slammed into the king and pinned him to the ground with her tail, her sharp claws poised over his throat. The man swallowed, his eyes twin pools of terror as he stared back at the daughter he had betrayed, at the daughter he'd refused to love and acknowledge.

The fighting ceased altogether, and it was as if everyone held in a collective breath. Watching. Waiting. Would Kikka take her revenge? Or would she show mercy?

"Do it!" her father hissed as he stopped struggling against her grip. "Show us all the monster you truly are. The monster I knew you were from the moment you sprouted your wings."

Kikka, Warren murmured softly in his mind, trying to bring her back to the present moment, to pull her out of her justifiable feral anger.

He took everything from me, she half-sobbed, half-screeched through their bond. *My family. My friends. My body. My voice. Ten years of my life. How can I possibly allow this man to live?*

Slowly, he lowered his hand and allowed his *iskra* to flicker out. If she did this, he feared it would blacken her heart forever. He knew her. She would never recover from this.

You are beautiful, Kikka. In body and soul. This man has hurt you. But don't give him the satisfaction of throwing away the light he never managed to steal. I love that light. He swallowed, his breath shuddering nervously from his lips as he spoke the one truth he knew without a shadow of a doubt in his heart. *I love* you. *And I know you are stronger than this.*

Kikka turned her head toward him, the yellow of her eyes harboring disbelief as she returned his stare. *No one has loved us for a very long time.*

He shook his head, gesturing to her brothers and mother. *They clearly love you. They are risking their lives for you. And I love you. You are the best thing to happen to me. Don't let me lose you.*

Not just in the physical sense. He didn't want to lose her good heart and kind soul, either.

After a few frosty breaths, her yellow eyes melded back into green. Her wings and claws retracted from her back and fingers.

And then slowly, her tail grew shorter and shorter until they formed two legs instead of one long limb.

She stood and took only a few steps away from her father.

But in her weaker form and dazed state of untransforming, she wasn't able to dodge fast enough when the king scrambled to his feet, dislodged a single arrow from his quiver, and slammed it downward.

Warren screamed with terror in his mind, delving deep into his *iskra* on instinct. He refused to lose someone else he loved to cruel, unjust humans. And this time, his magic obeyed his desire to protect as he used it to transport himself.

One moment, he lingered what seemed like leagues away. And the next, he stood in front of Kikka with arms outstretched.

Just as the arrow darted downward.

And stabbed him in the shoulder.

Warren felt the effects of the poison immediately. It coursed through his blood like hot coals. It seared and consumed and burned.

His breath faltered. His vision darkened. And unable to stand upright any longer, he collapsed into the frigid snow beneath him.

Warren! Horror stretched across Kikka's face as her bondmate collapsed in front of her. She reached for him, but her fingers only managed to brush his armor before the king grabbed her arm and flung her in the opposite direction.

She landed hard in the snow, the chilly powder kicking up around her and momentarily blinding her to his next attack. The king grabbed her again around the throat and lifted her close enough to see the anger swirling within the gray depths of his eyes.

He slid a second arrow out of his quiver, but before he could impale her with it, Jon tackled him off her and pinned him face first to the ground.

Kikka sputtered and gasped as she struggled for air. Her hazy vision focused enough to find her brother wrenching the king's arms behind his back and tying his hands tightly together.

Jon stood over their father now pinned by soldiers, a deep scowl on his face as he raised his voice to his men. "This man is unfit to rule. Forcing *others* to fight against their will. Attempting to murder his own daughter." He lifted his head and addressed his soldiers. "I am now Prince Regent."

"How dare you!" the king shouted, thrashing against his bonds, but the soldiers only held on tighter. "I am your father! I am the king! You have no right to rule."

"And I am your heir. I have found your mind sick. A mad king cannot sit on a throne and rule his people justly."

The king thrashed and snarled. "You won't sit on the throne for long. I'll make sure of it."

But Jon ignored the threat and addressed the soldiers. "Once we get him back to the palace, place him in the dungeons." And then he returned his glare to the king. "Don't worry, Father," he said snidely. "We'll make sure you are *comfortable.*"

As the soldiers dragged the king back toward their camp, Kikka scrambled through the snow, white powder flying around her, until she reached Warren's side.

His skin was pale. Raspy breaths escaped blue lips. Blood seeped through the cracks in his armor.

Warren! she screamed in her mind. *Warren!*

He didn't answer but winced when she grasped the shaft of the arrow sticking out of his shoulder.

That arrow was meant for me, she sobbed. *You can't take it. It's mine.*

Bracing her other hand against his chest, she pulled out the arrow in a swift movement and tossed it aside. Tears trailed down her face at the way he thrashed, the way he screamed, the sound forever imprinted in her mind.

The poison was killing him. It was meant for humans. He stood no chance against it.

Heal yourself! she demanded as she took both his hands and placed them over his chest. *You told me you can do it. So do it! Damn the consequences.*

Warren cracked his bloodshot eyes open. He lifted his hands off his chest and instead placed his fingers against her throat. "Your happiness means more to me than my life," he rasped.

When she realized what he was going to do, she tried to jerk away but moved too slowly. His *iskra* shot into her neck, the force of the magic throwing her backward into the snow. For a moment, her vision flashed white, and her ears rang. She gasped in each breath, fighting for her vision as she rolled back onto her hands and knees.

Little by little, her vision returned as swirling black dots before the image of her surroundings melded together to show her mother at Warren's side with her two brothers. She poured something over his wound, but he was too unconscious to release another scream or even a wince.

Don't hurt him! Her lips formed the words, but even as she tried to speak them out loud, her throat was unable to function correctly. Even after Warren tried to heal her, she wasn't sure it had worked. Rather, his efforts seemed to be killing him faster than the poison was.

"An antidote," her mother explained as she dabbed the remainder of the liquid around his open wound with a cloth. Her thin eyebrows furrowed as she focused on the task. "He will recover from this. We got to him fast enough."

Then why is he still dying? she tried to ask with hand gestures and pointing. Although her mother stared blankly at her, Aiden seemed to understand what she was trying to ask.

He knelt beside them, one knee in the snow as he frowned down at Warren. "The antidote is ridding him of the poison. But it can't heal him from his own stupidity." The man released a shaky breath. "He knows better than to attempt to heal someone. I don't know yet if he will make it through this."

Aiden and Koa grabbed Warren beneath the arms and hefted him off the ground, held aloft between the two of them before Gael quickly joined them. Koa nodded toward her, "We'll take him somewhere safe." He glanced uneasily at her family and the soldiers at their beck and call. "What will you do, Kikka?"

I'm coming.

She stood and gripped Warren's cold fingers tight in hers. Each breath he took was shallow and raspy as if he struggled with each inhale.

And then in a single blink of her eye, the Umazi warriors each used their *iskra* to transport them back to the fortress in a flash of white light.

Why did you do this? she cried in her head, her beast wailing with fear as they placed Warren in the infirmary for a second time. The man had saved her life. But he could still die. It was no wonder the Umazis never healed anyone. The attempt was killing Warren.

She touched her maimed throat, her chest tight as she fought off the panic and heartache lingering just out of reach. It seemed as if Warren's sacrifice was in vain.

"Kikka," Aiden called softly from across the infirmary. She lifted her head from where it rested on the edge of the cot to find the man lingering in the doorway, gesturing for him to follow her into the hallway.

With one last look at Warren's pale face, she reluctantly left his side after hours of holding his hand and begging him to survive and joined Aiden. But rather than stopping to speak with her, he led her down several corridors and into the commons...

Where her mother and brothers were waiting.

She froze mid-step, her chest tightening when she glanced between the three of them. Why were they here? To take her back and finish the job they'd attempted from the beginning?

But she relaxed—if only slightly—when she realized Aiden wouldn't have let them inside the fortress if he didn't trust them. As she glanced around the room, she noted it was absent of palace soldiers. They must have come alone without the threat of the army on their doorstep.

Aiden grimaced apologetically. "Without Warren, we have no way to translate for you, Kikka. They would like to speak to you, nonetheless."

She warily eyed the empty seat adjacent to her mother's. She hadn't spoken to these people in ten years. They'd abandoned her whether or not they'd truly known what was going on.

When she still didn't take a seat, her mother stood, wringing her hands as she spoke first. "Please forgive us. All we wanted was for you to live a normal life. Your father said he could take out your beast and keep you alive in the process." She lowered her gaze to the floor. "One year turned into two. Two into three. And before we knew it, ten years had passed. I should have intervened. I just…held onto the hope that you could be cured."

Her beast rattled in agitation.

I don't need a cure.

But her words fell on deaf ears.

Jon spoke next. "We want you to return home. Echidna or not, you belong with us."

Kikka shook her head and stepped backward. She cast a distressed glance toward Aiden, begging for his help but not knowing how to ask.

Thankfully, he seemed to understand her hesitation. "She and Warren have bonded. They are as good as married. She won't leave him."

She held up her hand to show off the black and white tattoo etched onto her ring finger. A promise of a future filled with happiness. She had everything she'd ever wanted right here in the fortress, and she didn't need anything more.

Jon frowned. "Are you sure?"

Her eyes flashed yellow as she gestured to herself, trying to tell them that she was an *other*, and she belonged with people like her. The moment she'd turned eleven years old, and her echidna had manifested, she no longer belonged in the palace.

Releasing a long, melancholy sigh, her mother lifted her gaze and managed a smile. "May we visit you? You aren't too far from the palace. And we still want you in our lives."

Again, Kikka hesitated. The moment they'd betrayed her, she'd forsaken them. She didn't want them in her life anymore. It hurt too much. Especially when no one had bothered to visit her in captivity. Almost as if they hadn't wanted to believe the truth.

But…

Perhaps they could still make amends and close the monumental chasm separating them. It could possibly make things hurt a little less.

Therefore, she pinched her fingers together to try to convey *sometimes*, and then mimicked writing a letter.

Her mother nodded. "We will write to you to seek permission each time. I only hope you might one day forgive us. Forgive *me*." She held out her arms, her hands shaking as if terrified of her reaction. "Will you allow me to embrace you?"

Kikka blinked rapidly, swallowing the hurt gathered from years of torment and heartache. For so long, all she'd wanted was a warm, loving embrace. For ten long years, she'd never received one.

With a nod, her mother pulled her into her arms, and Kikka couldn't help the twin trails of tears falling from her eyes as she hugged her back. Things were not all right. Perhaps they would never be all right again. The trust and love were gone. But this was a good start on the path toward healing.

They pulled away from one another, and Kikka offered her a watery smile as she wiped her eyes. If Warren recovered, if he lived through the invisible blade of his magic, then perhaps her family, minus her father, would come to her wedding ceremony.

Unable to remain in their presence for long when her mate was on the sickbed, she backed away slowly, offering an apologetic smile, before rushing toward the infirmary. Warren would make it through this. She knew it in her heart.

He would survive.

He was in the infirmary.
Again.

Familiar fatigue pressed heavy on Warren's body, telling him he'd accidentally dipped into his own life's energy from trying to use his *iskra* to heal another. He could not separate the two. No Umazi could.

Out of all the years Warren had trained as an Umazi warrior to perfect his weapons skills and his *iskra*, he could count on three fingers how many times he'd woken up in the infirmary in need of medical attention. Two of those times had been since he'd met Kikka.

But…

Until now, he'd never wanted to protect someone so fiercely. Without a second thought for himself. She was worth sacrificing for. She was his everything.

Tender fingers touched his cheek, and he turned his head to find Kikka smiling at him, the relief evident in her eyes from where she lay on the cot curled up next to him.

You can't make a habit of this, she teased through their bond.

His heart fell. He squeezed his eyes shut and released a despondent breath. "Why aren't you speaking? Did my healing not work? Please tell me my efforts weren't in vain."

Kikka touched her throat and sadly shook her head. *There is nothing there for you to heal.* But then she managed a confident smile as she lowered her hand to touch Warren's arm. *I am whole. Complete. I don't need my voice to make friends and communicate with others. To find myself a wonderful mate.* She kissed him affectionately on the cheek. *I am content with being exactly how I am, and I don't need you to risk your life in an attempt to fix me.*

"You never needed to be fixed." He lifted a weak hand and ran his fingers through the length of her wavy strands. "You are perfect the way you are."

Because he'd fallen in love with Kikka just the way she was. He'd wanted to give her everything, to give her what she deserved. He was only disappointed it hadn't worked. But if she was content with her lot… So was he.

She turned her head and kissed his palm. *Don't ever try to heal me again. Promise me.*

A weak chuckle escaped him as he nodded. "I thought the poison was going to kill me, anyway. But you're right. I should not have acted so rashly. Therefore, I give my promise."

Disappointment beat against his pounding skull when she climbed off the cot, taking her warmth with her as she crossed the room toward one of the tables. Needing to be near her, he sluggishly pulled the sheets off him and pushed himself to his feet, trying to keep himself steady when his head pounded with every passing second.

But Kikka noticed and gave him a warning rattle.

He couldn't stop himself from laughing as he wrapped a blanket around his shoulders and followed her across the room. She measured him with a watchful gaze as if making sure he wouldn't fall and injure himself before she turned her attention back to the blank sheet of parchment lying on the table next to a quill and ink.

There is another thing I want your help writing. She tapped the feather of her quill against the parchment. *It's very important.*

"Of course." He approached the desk in a few short strides. "I'm always happy to help. What do you want to spell?"

She lifted her face, her eyes shining like two radiant stars hanging in the midnight sky. *I love you.*

For a single moment, it felt as if his heart stopped when he realized she meant the words for him. He reached out and wrapped the blanket around her to trap her inside with him before leaning in for a gentle kiss.

"I love you, too," he murmured, sighing with happiness that his life was exponentially better with her in it. "From the very first moment I held you in my arms, I knew you were someone special. Thank you for giving me so much happiness."

Her finger tapped against his bottom lip as she smiled. *I never knew life could be so blissful. You've brought* me *so much happiness.*

Ussss, her beast corrected.

They laughed, Kikka playfully rolling her eyes, though not without a smile stretched across her face. *Us,* she agreed before she grabbed a fistful of his shirt and pulled him down for another kiss, and he happily obliged.

CHAPTER *Thirteen*

"I'M UNBELIEVABLY NERVOUS."

Warren's breath shuddered with each exhale as he buttoned his dark blue vest and straightened the sleeves of his white tunic peeking beneath. Nearly the entirety of the fortress—as well as Kikka's mother and five siblings—had shown up to witness the nuptials, now standing on luscious grass beneath the shade of multiple trees in the orchard. Each spoke excitedly over springtime birdsong and gentle winds, lively energy snapping tight in the air around them.

"Why?" Gael laughed as he slapped Warren on the back of the shoulder, his grin stretching wide across his face and pulling on his scar. He was dressed in a similar outfit but with a red vest instead of blue. It was the same with Koa, Aiden, and several other men. "You are already bonded to the woman. She's not going to reject you." He grinned teasingly. "Probably."

Rolling his eyes, Warren socked his friend in the shoulder. "Maybe *you* should be the nervous one," he teased as he tried to ignore the anxiety flipping through his stomach. "We all know how she liked to hiss at your advances. I wonder if she'll hiss at you today."

Rather than seeming offended, his friend only grinned. "Let's make this harder on your bride, shall we? Let's switch vests to confuse her sense of smell."

Despite his nerves, he laughed as he imagined Kikka blindingly choosing Gael to stand with her under the wedding arch. Of course, it was only a silly tradition, but amusing, nonetheless.

They traded vests before the group of them stood in a straight line, each quiet and still. The audience also quieted moments before Cyra's gold and red feathers moved into his line of sight, followed by Aspen's wooden limbs and fluttering leaves. Next, Enara stepped out of the trees, her newly grown black feathers stirring in the breeze. She pulled Kikka along by the hand, and the moment his bride stepped into view…

Warren's heart skipped in his chest, his pulse thrumming alive as his gaze raked over Kikka's light, fluttery blue gown as graceful as wildflower meadows singing beneath afternoon sunshine. Not once had he seen her wear a dress, but the sight of her stole his breath away. The fabric hugged her in all the right places. The sheer sleeves accentuated the grace of her arms and the gentle curve of her shoulders. Her hair was braided back with flowers neatly tucked into the woven strands. And then a blindfold rested over her eyes as the other three led her in his direction.

He smiled as he watched her nostrils flare as she took in the scents around her, as if she were trying to orient herself when she couldn't use her eyes as her guide.

Where are you? Kikka asked in his mind. *Tell me so I won't make a fool of myself.*

Reflexively, he opened his mind to answer, but Aiden silently pointed a warning finger at him as if to say, "No cheating allowed."

Rather than responding, he sent her a flood of reassurance and admiration through their bond before quieting himself once more.

Her adorable mouth quirked to the side as Enara led her to the front of the audience before abandoning her to her senses. She stood only an arm's length away from Koa, her nostrils flaring again as if taking in his scent in search of Warren.

A grin stretched across his face, and the audience laughed as she grimaced with disgust at Koa and shook her head at him.

"What?" Koa finally spoke, clearly feigning hurt through his laughter. "Don't you dare say I stink. I bathed this morning!"

More laughter, and it took all his effort to keep quiet himself.

For many *others*, this tradition was easier for them rather than for humans when many could use heightened senses to their advantage. Humans often had to resort to touching the lineup of men to locate their groom. And if they chose wrong? Well, it made for an amusing ceremony.

Kikka slowly shuffled to her right, skipping over Aiden and another shifter entirely before stopping in front of Gael. She inhaled once before her beast rattled excitedly. The audience laughed. Warren bit his tongue to keep from joining in.

She grabbed a fistful of Gael's vest and pulled him closer. But then she stiffened. Her mouth contorted into a snarl. Her fangs elongated in her mouth.

And then she hissed before pushing Gael away.

Warren slapped a hand to his mouth but couldn't stop his laughter from leaking through this time. Kikka's head darted in his direction, and all at once, her claws retracted, her fangs disappeared, and her mouth softened into a smile.

I don't like Gael's scent on you, she murmured through their connection as she latched onto him next and confidently pulled him into a kiss. The crowd roared with excitement, but all the noise seemed to fade away when her kiss sparked a pleasant heat through his body, when the feeling of her in his arms made him feel safe and secure and happy.

For a long time, he'd never thought he could be happy again. But after meeting Kikka... She brought so much happiness to his life, so much hope and warmth and joy. Now, he couldn't imagine his life without a beautiful, winged serpent by his side.

They broke the kiss, and he reached behind her head and gently untied the blindfold. When the long piece of fabric fluttered to the ground, it revealed the sparkle of mirrored joy shining back at him through green eyes.

"You found me." He brushed his thumb along her jaw.

I will always find you. She turned her head and kissed his palm.

Her beautiful gaze held him captive, making it difficult to tear his attention away when Aiden stepped forward to lead the ceremony. Warren and Kikka clasped hands, gazing lovingly at each other as Aiden spoke of the sanctity of bonding in the Umazi culture, at the permanent fusion of two souls. When he reached the part where they were to speak vows to one another, he started choking up before even saying them aloud.

He squeezed her hands. "Kikka, you are one of the strongest souls I know. I knew it long before we bonded our souls together, long before I could hear your thoughts and your dreams and your aspirations for the future. You have endured so much, and you are stronger because of it." He paused to wipe his eyes with the hem of his sleeve, but when Koa produced a white, square handkerchief, the audience chuckled while Warren took a moment to compose himself.

Taking a deep breath, he continued his vows, "You are beautiful inside and out, and I hope that I can somehow manage to give you as much happiness as you give me. I vow to love you, cherish you, and lift you when life gets rough. This I promise for the rest of my days."

Usss, her beast interrupted with an impatient rattle.

He laughed and gave Kikka's hands another squeeze. *The both of you. Always.*

But then his heart fell when she blinked rapidly, her fingers touching her maimed throat. Her words shook as she spoke them through his mind. *As a little girl, I went to plenty of weddings. I always dreamed of wearing a beautiful dress and speaking beautiful vows. I'm sad I can't do that.*

He brushed two errant tears away from her cheeks and leaned in to kiss her forehead. "It doesn't matter if you can't speak them out loud. I can still hear them."

I want all my friends to hear them as well.

Oh, how he wished he could heal her. To give her the power to speak. But his power had limits, and he wouldn't go against Kikka's wishes by attempting the feat again.

I can relay what you say to the audience.

Speaking yours and *my vows?* The suggestion inspired the faintest smile to lift on her lips. *It's unlike any wedding I've ever attended.*

He kissed a lone tear away that clung to her cheek. *Then it will be unique. Just like our union.*

After releasing a shaky breath, she nodded.

Addressing the audience, he said, "I will be speaking her vows. I'm sure I will butcher it, so bear with me."

As she spoke the vows in his mind, he repeated them out loud, "Warren, the first time we met, I hadn't known kindness in a long time. You held me when my legs couldn't stand on their own. You sacrificed your own warmth for me, even though you likely needed it more. You kept me tucked against your chest, safe in your arms. *Forever* safe in your arms."

Warren lost all composure as he released a choked sob, swiping the moisture from his eyes once again. It proved difficult to continue when she spoke such sweet, endearing words. But with a gentle squeeze from her fingers, he found the strength to continue.

He repeated, "You gave me my life. My freedom. My strength and my joy. I cannot fathom drawing a single breath without you in my life. You are everything to me." He swiped at his cheeks again. "And I will love and cherish you for the rest of my life."

Several people sniffed in the audience, and he, himself, couldn't manage to keep his eyes dry. Out loud, he jested, "You should have warned me you planned on speaking so sweetly."

Kikka's eyes sparkled with amusement. *But then you would have been too prepared for what I had planned to say.*

Aiden continued, "Because you have already spoken the words to bind your souls, I will now officially pronounce you husband and wife."

A burst of happiness sparked through their shared bond as they bound themselves together for a second time, but in a more official sense. Warren gently cradled her face in his hands and pulled her into a kiss while the crowd roared and clapped and whistled around them. Kikka smiled against his lips, and he couldn't help but smile back.

You are our light and joy, Kikka said in their minds, her beast rattling happily within her. *We are so glad we found you.*

I wouldn't have it any other way.

And then he kissed her again. Because just one kiss wasn't enough to convey how much she meant to him, how much he wanted to spend the rest of his life with her. He loved her. Beast, scars, and all. And he truly wouldn't have it any other way.

ABOUT THE AUTHOR

Sydney Winward is an award-winning fantasy and paranormal romance author who dabbles in the occasional historical fiction. She loves building complex worlds filled with magic, strong characters, and emotional stories that can make you laugh and cry.

Sydney is the author of the Sunlight and Shadows Series and the best-selling Bloodborn Series, and when she's not writing, she's reading, thinking about stories, or going on adventures with her children. She lives in Utah with her husband and three amazing kids.

www.sydneywinward.com

www.ingramcontent.com/pod-product-compliance
Lightning Source LLC
Chambersburg PA
CBHW061541310726
48972CB00008B/2556